THE
LITTLE
CAPTAIN

PAUL BIEGEL was one of Europe's most acclaimed and best-loved storytellers, and the author of more than fifty books for children. Born in the Netherlands in 1925, he studied law but worked as a comic-strip writer before writing his first novel, *The Golden Guitar*, in 1960. He wrote at a rate of almost a book a year for nearly forty years, producing timeless fantastical tales of dwarves, princesses, witches, robbers and talking animals. *The Little Captain* was first published in 1970 and was Biegel's bestselling title. *The King of the Copper Mountains* and *The Gardens of Dorr* are also available from Pushkin Children's Books.

THE
LITTLE
CAPTAIN

PAUL BIEGEL

ILLUSTRATED BY CARL HOLLANDER

PUSHKIN CHILDREN'S

Pushkin Press
71–75 Shelton Street
London WC2H 9JQ

Text copyright © heirs Paul Biegel
Illustrations © Carl Hollander 1970

Original publication in Dutch by Gottmer, Haarlem, the Netherlands under
the title *De kleine kapitein*

Translation rights arranged by élami agency

'The Little Captain and the Seven Towers' and 'The Little Captain and the Pirate
Treasure' were translated from the Dutch by Patricia Crampton. Every effort has
been made to contact the owner of the rights to her translations. Please contact
Pushkin Press if you are the copyright holder.

The books in this edition were first published in English separately by J.M. Dent
as *The Little Captain* (1971), *The Little Captain and the Seven Towers* (1973), *The
Little Captain and the Pirate Treasure* (1980)

First published by Pushkin Press in 2022

This publication has been made possible with financial support from the
Dutch Foundation for Literature.

**N ederlands
letterenfonds
dutch foundation
for literature**

9 8 7 6 5 4 3 2 1

ISBN 13: 978-1-78269-337-6

Designed and typeset by Tetragon, London
Printed and bound by CPI Group (UK) Ltd, Croydon, CRO 4YY

www.pushkinpress.com

Contents

THE LITTLE CAPTAIN

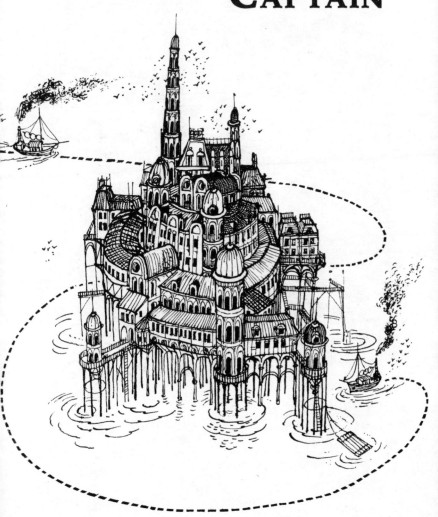

The Boat

The Little Captain lived on top of the dunes. Not in a house, not in a hut, but in a boat.

A raging storm which had blown the waves as high as skyscrapers had dashed the boat onto the dunes. And there she lay, stuck fast. Who had sailed in her no one knew. Only a boy had crawled up out of the cabin, a small boy wearing a big cap.

'Who are you?' asked the people from the harbour.

'The captain,' said the boy.

'Well, Little Captain,' said the old salt from the harbour, 'where do you come from?'

'From my boat,' replied the Little Captain.

'And where does your boat come from?'

But the Little Captain shrugged his shoulders and skipped back into his cabin.

He had lived there ever since.

When the sun shone he sat on the afterdeck and baked himself brown. When the moon shone he sat on the foredeck, playing his little brass trumpet.

Down in the harbour the people listened.

Ta-ran-ta-ra!

'It makes you go all soft inside,' the people said.

But the old salt thought it was beautiful.

Nobody knew where Salty had come from. If anyone asked him, 'from a shipwreck' was all he would reply.

One day he climbed the steep, sandy path to the top of the dunes to see the Little Captain.

'Would you like to come and live with us,' Salty asked.

The little boy shook his head.

'Why not?'

'I want to stay on my boat.'

'But it's a wreck.'

'I'm going to mend it,' said the Little Captain.

'And how will you get it back to sea again?' the old man inquired.

'I'll wait,' said the little boy. 'I'll wait for the next storm. And a wave. A back-to-front wave that will sweep my boat out to sea again.'

'I see,' said Salty, puffing on his pipe. 'And where will you sail?'

'To the island of Evertaller.'

'And what will you see there?'

'I don't know, whispered the little boy, 'but if only you can sleep there for one night, you will be a grown man when you wake up next morning.'

'Really?' Salty said. 'Are you sure?'

The Little Captain nodded. 'Yes, it takes so long to grow up here.'

'A very long time indeed,' the old man agreed. 'But do you know how to find this island of Evertaller?'

'No,' replied the Little Captain. 'I am searching for it. But first I will mend my boat.'

The old salt went home and the boy went down to the cabin to get his cart. It was made from an old chest with wheels underneath, but it ran rather crooked because one pair of wheels came from a bicycle and the other from a barrel-organ. It squeaked as the boy trundled it along, and when he passed through the streets of the little harbour town the people said: 'There goes the Little Captain.' They did not need to look; they could hear him.

The Little Captain piled everything he could find on the streets into his cart. A piece of stovepipe, a bit of rope, a baby's potty, some wire, a chair leg, a bicycle chain, a crooked nail, a length of tubing, a ball of wool, a broken mirror, a coin, an old shoe, a plank with two screws in it and a bit of fish-net.

And when one day he found a whistling kettle and an old bathtub he had all that he needed to build a new engine. He began to hammer and saw and beat and plane and he stuck his tongue out to help him as he worked. This engine had to be stronger than the storm waves.

But there were other children living in the small harbour town and, when they heard from the old salt about the island which the Little Captain meant to find, they all rushed up to the dunes, clambered on the deck of the boat and shouted: 'Little Captain, we want to grow up in one night too. Can we come with you?'

'Sure,' said the Little Captain. 'Just help me mend my boat.'

So Dicky and Podgy Plum and Marinka and the others helped. They pushed the bathtub up on the afterdeck where the engine was to be and began to hammer and saw and screw under the Little Captain's orders. The kettle here and the chair leg there, the bicycle chain up there, the pipe along there, and then the bathtub, upside-down, so that no steam could escape. In the end even Timid Thomas came and helped with the funnel, which was made of six buckets stuck one on top of the other.

'Thank you all very much,' said the Little Captain.

'When do we sail?' asked Podgy.

'When the big wave comes,' said the captain. 'But first we have to make the propeller.'

They were going to begin right away, but at that moment they heard voices in the dunes. The people from the town had missed their children, who should have been going to school.

They advanced with great strides up the steep, sandy path, the teacher at their head. He was flourishing his stick angrily.

The Great Wave

The fathers and mothers came panting up the steep path after the master. When they reached the Little Captain's boat at the top, they began to shout: 'Hey, Dicky! Hey, Marinka! Come here, you must go to school at once!'

The teacher banged on the side of the boat with his stick.

The children hung over the rail and called back: 'We don't have to go to school any more! We're going to the island of Evertaller to learn everything in one night and then we will be grown-ups!'

'I never heard such rubbish!' cried the schoolmaster sternly. 'Who told you that?'

'The Little Captain,' said the children.

'Ha!' shouted the master, turning as red as a lobster. 'And where is this island to be found?'

'We don't know,' cried the children. 'We are going to look for it.'

'I'll teach you to look for it!' shouted the master. In one bound he was on deck, chasing the children off the boat with his stick. 'I'll teach you where to find the island of Evertaller!' he cried. 'Off to school with you!'

It was a dismal procession, but Timid Thomas was not in it. He was quaking with fright, hidden away in the hold.

The Little Captain leaned over the rail, staring after the children. He did not have to go to school; the master and the fathers and mothers could not tell him what to do. No one could tell the Little Captain what to do. He picked up his brass trumpet and began to play the song of the sea:

> 'O sea, O sea,
> Set my little boat free!
> She lies all alone where the dunes are dry—
> Send us a wave as high as the sky.'

After this song the Little Captain suddenly thought of the propeller he had to make. A bronze propeller, stronger than the waves. He took his cart and his brass trumpet and went down to the town. He laid his cap on the ground, put the trumpet to his lips and began to play.

Ta-ran-ta-ra!

The people came out and stayed to listen, because the Little Captain played so that the music went in at your ears and straight down to your heart. He didn't play jazz and he didn't play pop, but he played the song of the endless sea—of happy mermaids and mournful gulls. And in between the songs he would call from time to time: 'A penny for the trumpeter!'

After an hour his cap was full of pennies. He tipped them into his cart, moved a few streets farther on and began again, until his cart was brimming over with pennies.

Then he pushed it carefully back to his boat.

After school the children came back. The Little Captain said: 'Go and find some drift-wood. We have to melt this heap over a hot fire.'

'Why?' asked the children.

'To make a propeller,' said the Little Captain.

The boys and girls collected wood from the beach and the Little Captain threw the pennies into his iron saucepan. The fire blazed up and made the pan glow like the sun. Podgy Plum and the others danced round it, but the Little Captain was digging in the sand. He was making the shape of a propeller which would be stronger than the waves and he beat the sand into shape with the flat of his hand.

'Hurrah!' cried the children when the money had melted and the red-hot bronze was bubbling. It sounded like *Ta-ran-ta-ra!*

Then the Little Captain took seven oven-cloths, grasped the pan and poured the bronze into the hollow in the sand. It hissed and spluttered and the sparks flew. The children drew back, all but Timid Thomas who was still in the hold, peeping out through the hatch.

Up came Salty. He spat on the bronze to see if it sizzled. 'Still as hot as an iron,' he said. But after an hour it had cooled down.

They dug the bronze propeller out of the sand. The three blades glittered in the sun and the sailor tapped it with his pipe. 'It sings like a mermaid,' he said, and together they fixed the propeller to the boat. Then they brightened her name up with fresh paint: *Neversink*.

'Perhaps you will bring them all back with you,' said Salty.

'Who?' asked the Little Captain.

But the old man turned away without answering and walked back to the harbour.

Now the Little Captain's ship was ready to sail. They were only waiting for the great wave, the back-to-front wave which was to pluck the ship from the dune top and sweep it out to sea.

'Will you call us?' asked the children.

'Yes,' said the Little Captain.

But then the parents came back and dragged their children home: they were not allowed to sail away with the Little Captain. They were not allowed to sail to the island of Evertaller, because it did not exist, said their parents. The Little Captain leaned over the rail, staring after them.

Then the wind began to blow. Harder and harder, so hard that the Little Captain began to stoke the fire under the steam kettle. The wind made the flames roar and the six-bucket funnel shuddered. In the middle of the night the waves flung themselves upon the dune top like baying hounds. 'The big one's coming,' thought the Little Captain. He stood on the afterdeck blowing his trumpet to summon the other children. But the children were sleeping in their warm beds, dreaming that they were on the island already. All except Podgy and Marinka. They sprang to their feet and rushed out. Their night clothes fluttered in the gale and the spray spattered their faces. They ran to the top of the dune, barefoot in the wet sand.

'We're coming!' they cried.

But their voices were smothered by a deafening uproar. A giant breaker reared up, tall as a tower, and, just as Podgy and Marinka grasped the rail, the boat was caught up and swept out to sea.

Out into the wild, desolate sea.

Popinjay Port

The waves were fiercer than wild beasts. They flung themselves on the boat and seemed to be roaring: '*Neversink?*
We'll get you!' The Little Captain stood at the helm, sure
and steady. His shoes might have been nailed to the deck.
He said nothing, only steered. Podgy and Marinka were
still hanging onto the rail, their night clothes fluttering
like flags.

'Landlubbers!' shouted the Little Captain. 'Stoke the
fires, look lively!' Then Podgy suddenly had to laugh.
He brushed the sea-spray from his face and did not feel
frightened any more. He and Marinka crawled to the
afterdeck and together they heaped the black coals on
the flames and poked the fire.

Thick black clouds of smoke belched from the six-
bucket funnel: the engine began to bellow louder than
the storm and the propeller roared more savagely than
the waves. So the ship with its three-child crew forged
its way through the stormy seas to a region far beyond,
where the sea was calm and the sun stood high in
the sky.

Then they heard a pounding on the hatch. A wailing
voice issued from the hold: 'I want to go home!'

The Little Captain unscrewed the storm battens and opened the hatch. The small, white face of Timid Thomas came into view, peering anxiously about.

'Oh, I do hope we won't drown!' he cried.

The sea was so huge.

'Of course we won't,' said the Little Captain.

'How on earth did you get here, sailor hero?' asked Podgy.

But Marinka cried: 'What does that matter? He'll be useful to swab the decks.'

'That's right,' said the Little Captain. 'He is a stowaway. He can be our deck-hand.'

'Can I come to the island with you?' asked Timid Thomas. 'Where you get big?'

'Certainly not,' said Podgy. 'You're not allowed to land. You must stay on board and mind the ship.'

They sailed on for four days. Timid Thomas swabbed the decks, Podgy stoked the fire and Marinka baked pancakes. Sometimes one would fall in the sea, and then two codfish came and gobbled it up. But the Little Captain just stood at the helm, sure and steady, and steered with his eyes on the horizon.

At night they slept in the cabin, side by side in hammocks, swinging gently to and fro. And if Thomas cried because he wanted to go home, Marinka muttered: 'Quiet, cry-baby!' but the Little Captain steered, his feet firmly planted on the deck, his eyes on the stars.

On the fifth day Marinka climbed the mast (because

Podgy was too fat and Thomas too frightened) and cried: 'Land ahead!'

'We'll go there,' said the Little Captain, and they sailed into Popinjay Port. Timid Thomas wanted to go ashore too and he followed the others, rolling like a real seaman.

The people of Popinjay looked like a lot of parrots, because they loved to dress in red and green and yellow clothes.

'How pretty,' said Marinka.

Then the Little Captain took his trumpet and began to play.

Podgy went round with the cap and Marinka sang:

> 'Popinjay parrots are happy and bright
> Oh, what a gaudy, glorious sight!
> Bright as a banner and ever so jolly—
> Throw us a penny for Popinjay Polly.'

The people clapped their hands and threw so many coins into the cap that Podgy was able to buy a green jacket and red trousers and Marinka a dress as beautiful as a butterfly. Timid Thomas got a cap with a long tassel and a bell on the end.

'So that we can hear you if you run away,' said Podgy.

Then the Little Captain went into the big sailors' home to ask the way to the island of Evertaller. He found five hulking sailors in bell-bottom trousers and they all laughed at him. The bellows of their laughter reached

the top floor, where the old lighthouse-keeper sat. He came downstairs. He did not laugh about the island of Evertaller, but took the Little Captain up with him and pointed across the wide sea.

'Yonder,' said he, 'where my light shines at night, three days off, is the stone dragon gate. If you were to pass through it you would come to the island. But put about at once, because you cannot pass.'

'Why not?' asked the Little Captain.

'The dragon gate is only made of stone at night,' said the lighthouse-keeper. 'But then it is so dark that you will run onto a rock.'

'And by day?' asked the Little Captain.

'By day,' said the lighthouse-keeper, 'by day you cannot pass.'

'Why not?' asked the Little Captain again.

'By day the gate is not made of stone.'

'Oh?' said the Little Captain. 'What is it made of, then? Dragons?' But the lighthouse-keeper turned away and gave no answer.

'Go back,' was all he said.

'Thank you,' said the Little Captain and he went down to where the others stood waiting.

'Do you know the way?' they asked.

'Yes,' said the Little Captain.

So they bought more coal and ten bags of dough for the pancakes. They loaded it on the cart and made Thomas pull it.

Half an hour later the *Neversink* put out to sea. A butterfly and a parrot joined the children hanging over the rail and a bell tinkled on Thomas the deck-hand's cap.

The Little Captain steered straight for the place where the lighthouse beam pointed after the sun had set.

The Dragon Gates

After three days the Little Captain called: 'Anchor aweigh!'

'Why?' asked Podgy Plum.

'Anchor aweigh!' commanded the Little Captain again, sure and steady like a grown-up captain.

Podgy let the chain rattle out and the *Neversink* sat bobbing up and down on the open sea.

'We can't go any farther until it is dark,' explained the Little Captain.

'Are we near the growing island then?' asked Marinka, dancing over the deck like a butterfly. 'I hope my dress grows with me.'

'First we have to go through the stone dragon gates.'

Timid Thomas dropped the mop with a clatter. 'Dragon gates?' he asked, trembling.

'They're stone!' declared the Little Captain. 'I told you—the dragons are made of stone! At least,' he added, 'they're stone at night.'

'D-do we have to go through b-big black gates in the d-dark?' asked Thomas.

'Full of monsters that tear you to pieces!' shouted Podgy.

'And pull your hair!' cried Marinka.

'I want to go home!' wailed Thomas, frightened.

But Marinka said to him cheerfully: 'Here, have a pancake. That will make you brave.' She tossed the pancake high and it did a fine somersault in the air but plopped into the sea. The two codfish were still swimming alongside and they gobbled it up.

Marinka looked over the rail. 'Hey!' she called suddenly. 'There's something funny about these fish. They keep circling round the boat as if to say: "Don't go on." '

But the sun went down and on they sailed.

'Look at that!' shrieked Podgy.

There, straight ahead, in the glimmering dusk, a gloomy black rock rose out of the sea, like a wall. But the Little Captain sailed on.

Then they saw the dragons. Two monsters as high as houses stood on their hind legs facing each other, the claws of their forepaws locked together to form a gate. Their jaws hung wide open and their tongues seemed to quiver in the rosy evening light. It looked as if they were still moving.

'Full speed ahead!' shouted the Little Captain.

Podgy threw fresh coal on the fire; but Marinka stopped dancing and Timid Thomas crept into the hold.

It was pitch black under the gate. The beacon from the lighthouse of Popinjay Port did not reach this far and the Little Captain could no longer see the bows of the ship.

'Half speed!' he called.

But before Podgy could damp down the fire, the ship shivered to a stop. The *Neversink* had hit an under-water rock and lay grounded.

'Ooh!' squealed Marinka.

'What now?' asked Podgy.

'We're going down!' yelped Timid Thomas, scrambling through the hatch.

But the Little Captain, undaunted, said: 'The tide will lift us.'

They settled down to wait. All around them was silence—a great, empty, eerie silence. The only sound was the lapping of the water against the stone claws of the dragons. The children couldn't see them, and that made it all the more creepy. The Little Captain picked up his trumpet and began to play. The notes struck the stone bellies of the beasts and there was such an odd echo that even Timid Thomas had to giggle.

But when the grey light of morning came, the boat still lay fast. The tide wasn't high enough. The sun peeped over the horizon and began to warm the stone dragons.

Slowly they came to life. First their tongues and then their heads. They started to growl and roar, and as soon

27

as their throats were warm the whole gate shuddered with the monsters' coiling and writhing—their top halves were alive.

Thomas yelled.

Podgy turned white.

Marinka hid her face in her hands.

The Little Captain looked over the rail, and he saw the water churning and seething—with codfish! Not just two, but two with a hundred of their friends. And all hundred and two pulled the boat off the under-water rock so that it could sail away.

'Double speed ahead!' cried the Little Captain.

Podgy threw a whole bucket of coal on the fire at once and the *Neversink* shot over the waves and began to pass between the dragons. By this time the dragons were alive down to their bellies. They growled and snorted and spat fire.

'Into the cabin!' ordered the Little Captain.

Thomas had been there for a long time already. Podgy and Marinka dived in too. But the Little Captain stayed at the helm, sure and steady, his eyes fixed on the horizon, where he could see the island of Evertaller rising out of the sea.

By the time the *Neversink* emerged beyond them the dragons were alive right down to their knees. They lunged forward trying to seize the boat, and scrabbled with their claws as far as they could reach.

The Little Captain never looked back.

The Island of Evertaller

'I see giants!' squealed Timid Thomas.

He tried to take refuge in the cabin again, but the Little Captain held him back. 'No you don't, they're just trees,' he said, because the *Neversink* now lay off the island of Evertaller.

'I see witches!' screeched Thomas, struggling to escape.

'No you don't, they are flowers,' said the Little Captain.

'I don't want to go there,' stammered Thomas.

But the Little Captain steered towards an inlet. It was a narrow passage between two high cliffs. 'Half speed!' he called to Podgy, thinking there might be under-water rocks.

But there were no rocks and the *Neversink* steamed steadily into a lagoon as calm as a goldfish pond. Podgy

Plum was the first to land and he started prancing around like a circus elephant.

> 'Hip-hip-ho-ho!
> Just watch me grow!'

'Don't make so much noise—there may be monsters!' called Timid Thomas, who was still cowering as far away as he could on the afterdeck.

'So what!' cried Marinka leaping light as a butterfly to the shore. 'Once they've eaten Podgy Plum they won't have any appetite left for us.'

'There aren't any cannibals,' said the Little Captain. He clambered ashore with a rope and made the boat fast to a tree.

'Thomas!' shouted Podgy. 'You'd better stay on board to fight off the pirates!'

'Pirates?' shrieked poor Thomas. He plunged through the hatch into the hold and slammed the hatch cover shut after him.

'Sleep tight!' called Podgy.

They went to have a look around, because before you go to sleep on an uninhabited island, you ought to find out if it really is uninhabited. That's what the Little Captain said, and he went on ahead.

They discovered trees as high as church steeples and flowers as big as sunshades and shells like tents; but not a house nor a hut nor a path. Nor were there any footprints of cannibal or pirate.

'It really is uninhabited,' declared Podgy.

But just as he said these words, he bumped his nose against the Little Captain's cap, and Marinka bumped her nose against Podgy's back, for the Little Captain had come to a sudden halt.

'Look at that,' he said.

They looked. On the ground lay a pocket-watch.

'Giants!' squeaked Marinka. Because the watch was bigger than a church clock. The children ran to hide in the bushes. Podgy didn't believe in giants, but his heart beat furiously. Who could own a watch that size? How big was he—and how strong? And where was he?

'Let's go,' whispered Marinka.

'No,' said the Little Captain. He walked briskly to the watch and took hold of the ring at the top. 'Come and help.'

The three of them managed to heave it up. Its silver back was dull and tarnished.

'It's been lying here for a long time,' said the Little Captain.

But when he rapped on it with his fist, it began to tick. Tick-tock. Tick-tock. It sounded a bit rusty. They plumped the watch down on the sand with its silver back uppermost and Marinka began to polish it with spit.

'Look at that!' she cried. There was one letter on it. An 'S'.

'Well,' said the Little Captain. 'It must belong to a sailor who was cast away here.'

'A sea giant?' asked Marinka.

'No,' said the Little Captain. 'But it must have been lying here for ages on the island of Evertaller, and here everything gets bigger and bigger.'

'Oh! And we'll keep on growing too?'

The Little Captain nodded. 'That's why we have to leave again tomorrow.'

'I'll say!' cried Marinka. 'Otherwise we'll be giants.'

Podgy wouldn't have minded or so he said. But then he thought about S, the castaway. If he hadn't been able to sail away, then he must still be somewhere on the island. And he must have grown to be a real giant...

'L-l-let's go,' said Podgy.

'No,' said the Little Captain. 'We have to search farther.'

They took each other by the hand, the Little Captain in the lead, and walked cautiously on through the enormous bushes and trees.

'Look at that!'

The Little Captain halted again. On the ground lay a chest, its sliding top half open, full of red painted wooden beams with round yellow tops. Matches! A giant box of matches.

'Also belonging to the shipwrecked sailor,' muttered the Little Captain. 'He could make a fire, and so can we.'

And the three children shoved the box to the shore near the boat, and gathered wood into a heap. Then Podgy held the box steady, the Little Captain struck a beam-match with all his strength and Marinka shielded the flame from the wind by holding out her wide butterfly skirt.

It was a fine fire and it burned the whole night. The light of the flames flickered on the faces of the three sleeping children as they dreamed a little uneasily about the giant sailor; it flickered on the boat in which a little boy hardly slept at all because he was afraid of pirates. And everything seemed to grow in the firelight.

By the morning they would be grown up. They would be grown-up people and sail home in their big ship and never have to go to school again.

If only it wasn't a real giant...

The Giant

The next morning, the sun rose early. It shone down on the trees of the island of Evertaller, casting long shadows. But the shadows soon grew shorter as the sun climbed higher in the sky.

Podgy woke up. He yawned, rubbed his eyes and peered around. He saw trees and flowers and in the distance a hill, all just as usual.

'Why were we so afraid yesterday evening?' he wondered.

Podgy stretched himself and turned over on the soft sand to have another nap. But instead he gave a yelp. Right in front of his nose stood a pair of enormous feet. The feet of a giant.

Podgy gave another yelp and jumped up. But what a long time it took to get up. And when at last he was on his feet, he felt as if he were looking out of a skylight.

'A giant, are you? Why, I'm one myself! Come on and fight!'

Then he saw that the other giant, who had given him such a fright, was the Little Captain.

'So you're awake at last!' said the little giant captain merrily.

'Yes,' roared giant Podgy. 'And it's true! We've grown!'

He began to prance around until the ground of the island of Evertaller shook.

But the island wasn't big any more. The whole world wasn't big any more. Podgy would never have to stand on tiptoe again when he tried to see over a crowd.

'Marinka!' he cried. 'Marinka, we've grown up!'

Giantess Marinka came strolling along with a bunch of wild flowers in her hands. And the hatch on the ship opened and out fell the giant deck-hand of the ocean liner *Neversink*. He was staggering around as if he felt dizzy.

'My head's much too high,' complained timid giant Thomas.

But Podgy took him by the hand and the three of them danced in a ring around the little giant captain.

> 'Hurrah for the captain and his ship!
> Hurrah for us giants! Skip, skip, skip!'

So they sang, and the Little Captain played a splendid fanfare on his trumpet.

Then Marinka said: 'Grown-ups don't dance around like this, so we can't be grown-ups. Huh, it's not true at all.'

She sat down daintily on a stone and began to comb her hair with her fingers and smooth her dress. Then she gave a sigh and said: 'What a sight I must look.'

Podgy stomped over to a tree, broke off a branch, and said: 'Shall we take a little walk?'

'Oh no, for goodness' sake,' cried Timid Thomas.

'That would be far too dangerous.' Though big, he was still not brave.

But the Little Captain said: 'We have to leave. Otherwise we'll grow too tall.'

'Ooh!' whispered Marinka. She looked at the Little Captain. He wasn't dancing and prancing around, but standing by himself, with his gallant cap on, and a look of the distant sea in his eyes. The giantess Marinka felt a strange warm glow inside her, and that was because she had fallen in love, just like a grown-up person.

'It's time to stoke the fire,' said the gallant captain. 'We must leave at once.'

Podgy and Timid Thomas went to look for firewood in the great forest.

'Watch how you go,' warned Thomas. 'You can't be too careful.'

'Let them all come!' said Podgy. He clenched his fists and strode ahead.

Podgy went off, gathering wood, until he came to a sandhill where he saw a thick root sticking out. 'That will burn well,' he thought, tugging to get it loose. Then he stiffened with surprise.

The sand moved and something came out of it. It was a toe—an enormous toe, as big as a man's fist.

Podgy dropped his bundle of firewood and stood trembling. The giant toe moved.

Podgy gave a yelp and took to his heels. 'A giant!' he squealed. 'A real giant.'

In thirty giant strides he was back at the boat and jumped aboard, the others after him.

From the island came a rumbling sound, something between thunder and a yawn. And the sandhill began to toss and turn like an earthquake.

'Quick!' screamed Marinka. 'Let's get away. Something's happening.'

Podgy grabbed the firewood that Thomas had collected, threw it on the ashes of the ship's fire and began to blow. The fire blazed up and there was a hiss of steam. The Little Captain stood at the helm. Thomas longed to hide in the hold, but he had to untie the rope that moored the ship.

Slowly the *Neversink* steamed across the lagoon towards the opening in the rocks.

'A giant!' shrieked Marinka. 'It's true! I can see him!' She pointed over the rail towards the sandhill, and now they could see that a man as high as a steeple had been lying half under the sand. He was sitting up, scratching his tousled hair, then he opened his mouth as wide as a cave, and gave another huge yawn, 'Aaaooh!'

The *Neversink* sped over the water towards the passage in the rocks. But just as they reached it the Little Captain ordered, 'Full speed astern!'

'What?' yelled Podgy, but at the same instant there was a crash. The boat lay fast, jammed between the rocks.

The *Neversink* had grown as well—she was too broad to get through.

'Aaaooh!' yawned the giant again.

The Rescue

Timid Thomas shot into the hold. Marinka clung to the Little Captain. Podgy, with his mouth open and his eyes bulging, gazed up, up, up at the great steeple of a man, with legs like tree trunks.

'Hey there, what's going on?' bellowed the giant.

'We're grounded,' replied the Little Captain.

'So I see,' said the giant. He came and sat at the edge of the water, with his feet in the lagoon as if in a tub. 'You're a fine captain, I must say. Zero marks for seamanship. Have you come to rescue me?'

'N-no,' said the Little Captain. 'We came to grow bigger.'

'Ha!' cried the giant. 'Well, now you can see what happens. Just take a look at me. You'll never get away again.'

'Oh... Won't we?' murmured the children.

'Why are you all looking so scared?' asked the giant. 'Do you think I'm a giant?'

They nodded.

'Ha, ha!' he bellowed. 'And I suppose you also think you're grown up?'

They nodded.

'Get away with you. You only grow tall here, that's all. I was washed up here years ago when I was shipwrecked. But I'm still just Gus, able seaman Gus: taller, but no different otherwise.'

'Oh,' said Podgy.

'And make no mistake—you're still just children,' said Gus.

'Oh,' said Marinka.

'But it's a good thing you've come,' exclaimed Gus. 'I've been longing to get away from here. Now we'll be able to leave the island.'

'How?' asked the Little Captain.

'With me on a raft,' answered Giant Gus. 'And you towing me behind you.'

'Fine,' said the Little Captain. 'If you can get us loose.'

Gus spat in the lagoon, bent over, gripped the *Neversink* firmly in his enormous fists, pulled her with a scraping sound from between the rocks, lifted her, crew and all, high in the air, and put her down gently in the open sea on the other side.

'There you are,' he muttered, spitting again into the water. 'Now for the raft. Give me a hand.'

Giant Gus began to uproot trees. He laid them neatly side by side in the sea. The Little Captain and Podgy lashed them together with ropes, making tight sailors' knots.

Marinka started making pancakes, a hundred for Gus and ten for each of the others, and Thomas stuck his head through the hatch and asked: 'What's happening?'

By afternoon the raft was ready. It was a hundred and twenty-seven trees wide—nearly as big as the lagoon that lay behind them.

Let's be off, fellows!' cried Gus. 'Hang on, have I forgotten anything? Ah yes, just a second.' He strode off and came back carrying something in his hand.

The watch,' cried Podgy.

You've got it,' said Gus. 'My mate's watch. I'll give it back to him—if I can find him again—because it's still keeping time.' He wound it, and it began to tick.

'Who is your mate?'

'He's the old salt with a grey beard,' answered Gus. 'Perhaps you know him?'

'Oh yes,' cried Marinka. 'He lives quite near us in the harbour. We call him Salty.'

'Salty,' nodded Gus. 'My best mate. There were seven of us. The old salt was our skipper and then there was me, Dirk and Max, Titch, Fred and Crooked Ben. All lost—in a shipwreck. Bah! But now I've been rescued at last. Thank you! Anchor aweigh! Take me back to Salty.'

And Podgy said: "Now I know what the letter S stands for.

Gus lay down cautiously on the raft. It held.

Then Podgy blew the fire into a blaze, until white steam hissed up the funnel. Thomas began to mop like mad, and busy Marinka made a new batch of pancakes. The Little Captain stood at the helm, sure and steady, and pulled on the steam whistle. Slowly the *Neversink* began to move. She made out to sea like a tugboat, pulling the huge raft after her, with the huge sailor lying snoring on top of it, saved from the island of Evertaller at last.

And as the island faded into the distance behind them, they stood and watched the red sun sinking into the sea. The Little Captain took his brass trumpet and began to play the tune of a happy song:

> 'The sun sinks in the sea,
> So hot it burns and frizzles,
> It's very odd, it seems to me,
> It never ever sizzles.'

Then they saw the dragon gate, and Thomas dropped the mop with a clatter.

'How do we get through it now?' asked Podgy.

But Giant Gus simply lifted the boat over it, and then the raft, and they sailed on.

'It's fine to be big, after all,' said Marinka as she tossed a pancake into the sea for the codfish. 'What tiny little darlings they look now,' she cried.

But the next day, the codfish swimming around the boat were bigger. And by the afternoon, they were bigger still and the next day they were enormous.

'What can be happening?' they exclaimed.

Gus's voice thundered from the raft; 'Silly kids, do you think you stay big, once you've left the island?'

It was true: the spell didn't last and they were children once again. The Little Captain's cap looked too big for his head, and Marinka didn't feel any glow inside when she looked at him.

And a few days later, just an ordinary man lay on the raft. An able seaman. 'Old shipmates Salty and Gus will soon be having a reunion,' he chortled.

But Podgy and Marinka were disgusted. They didn't feel at all like going to school again. They had had an adventure, but who would believe them? They weren't grown up after all. Thomas didn't want to go home, because he knew he would be in trouble. And the Little Captain?

The Little Captain stood at the helm, his eyes on the horizon, and wondered about old Salty's shipwreck. Had his other shipmates also been cast up on strange shores? Were they still alive? He altered course. There was no need to go straight back the way they had come.

The Mysterious Island

The *Neversink* sailed on for seven days. Since the adventure on the island of Evertaller nothing unusual had happened. Not one smudge of land on the horizon. Seven days of sea, sea, and more sea, and only the Little Captain's boat, with Gus's raft behind it.

Thomas wept. 'We're lost. We should have been home long ago.'

Marinka gave his ear a tweak. 'Cheer up, cry-baby, bring me a pan of water. I'm going to make some pancakes.'

The water-barrel was in the cabin, but it was empty.

'Boo hoo! What shall we do now?' Thomas sobbed more than ever.

'Nothing,' declared Podgy. 'Your salty tears certainly won't help, and neither will the sea, for that's salty too.'

Now Marinka couldn't bake any more pancakes, and there wasn't a drop of water to drink.

'I'm thirsty,' called Gus from the raft.

'I'm thirsty,' echoed Thomas.

Marinka and Podgy, their throats too dry to speak, said nothing, and the Little Captain sailed first to port and then to starboard searching for land where they could go ashore and find fresh water.

Podgy climbed the mast to see farther, and that was wise, for just as Gus croaked, 'I'm thirsty,' for the eleventh time, Podgy saw a tiny dot in the far distance.

'I see something!' he shouted.

'What kind of something?' asked Marinka hoarsely.

'I think it's land ... or no ... a mountain ... I mean ...'

'What do you mean?'

'An island!' exclaimed Podgy. 'There!'

The Little Captain steered where he pointed and after half an hour a strange island loomed up. It was a mountain without a peak, like a huge crown, covered with bushes and trees.

'It's a volcano,' said the Little Captain.

At once Thomas began to tremble. 'Is it going to erupt?' he asked.

'Of course,' said Podgy and Marinka, full of mischief, but the Little Captain called 'Stand by!' and brought the *Neversink* safely to the shore.

Even before they dropped anchor, Gus sprang off the raft and waded ashore. 'I'm thirsty,' he called and strode off to look for water.

'Hey, Gus!' shouted Podgy.

But the Little Captain said: 'Let's wait for him to come back. Then we won't have to search.'

Their throats parched, they waited. Five minutes. Ten minutes. Half an hour. They tried to shout, but you can't

shout very loud if your throat is dry. No answer came.
Only the seagulls crying and the breakers pounding the
beach.

The four small sailors decided to go ashore themselves
to look for water and for Gus.

'He's probably fallen into the volcano,' announced
Thomas. The Little Captain said nothing, but marched
ahead, following the footprints of the seaman in the sand.
On and on, until they disappeared into—

'Water!' cried Podgy.

The footprints vanished in a stream that came foaming down the mountain to the sea, making the sound of
a running tap.

Podgy plunged his head right under, Marinka cupped
her hands and drank from them, the Little Captain took
his cap off before drinking, and Thomas swallowed some
water the wrong way and choked. They drank until they
almost had stomach-ache, and then they lay on the grass.
Suddenly Podgy said: 'But what's happened to Gus?'

They looked for more footprints, but there were none.
They called, they shouted, but there was no sign of the
missing sailor.

'It's not possible,' said Podgy.

'He's climbed up the mountain to look inside the
volcano. That's what I think,' said the Little Captain.

'Into the fire?' asked Thomas anxiously.

The Little Captain shook his head. 'There isn't any
fire. There's something else inside. That's what I think.'

He put his cap on again. 'We must go and look for him,' he said.

But the hill was very steep. They followed the stream as far as they could, but when they tried to go farther they kept slipping on the boulders. Podgy almost twisted his ankle, and Thomas fell on his nose. Prickly thorns barred their way and any clear patches were too slippery to walk on. They went round the hill to try again a bit farther on, but they came to a river too wide to cross.

'Look at that,' said Podgy, hobbling behind the others because of his sore ankle. There was a tunnel in the side of the hill through which the river flowed down to the sea. 'Shall we go through there?'

But the Little Captain shook his head. 'We'd have to swim.'

'Let Timid Thomas have a try,' teased Marinka.

But the Little Captain shook his head again. 'No,' he said, 'the current's too strong. Even an able seaman couldn't manage it. Perhaps we can look through it though.'

They tried. The tunnel was like a telescope, but there wasn't much to see through it. They thought they could make out a valley on the other side, misty and mysterious. Podgy thought he could see houses, but Marinka said they were rocks, and Thomas was convinced they were great smoky flames.

But the Little Captain, who had turned away, suddenly exclaimed; 'Look! Down there.'

Where the river ran into the sea lay a wreck, an old wreck of an old ship, half buried in the sand.

Pirates?

The rusty old wreck lay in the mouth of the river, glistening with slimy seaweed. The wind howled through the holes in its sides. The Little Captain clambered up onto the lopsided deck and tried to find a way inside the ship. Podgy and Marinka crawled up after him. Rotted ropes and smashed chests lay all around.

'Hey!' cried Podgy. 'What does that say?'

Marinka bent over and tried to read the letters that sea and wind had almost wiped off one of the chests. 'CIR,' she read. 'What does it mean?'

'It's the name of the ship, of course,' said Podgy.

But then the Little Captain called, 'Come and help.'

He had found a door, and all three of them put their shoulders to it and pushed. 'One, two, three, hup!' They fell through it, and found themselves on a heap of canvas at the foot of some steps.

The darkness smelled stale and seemed full of little wriggly creatures. The floor was awash with water and in it squirmed crabs, jellyfish and shrimps.

'Funny. It smells like a stable,' said Podgy, puzzled.

'Watch out you don't get a stain on your new trousers,' warned Marinka, grinning.

'Never mind that, just look.' Podgy pointed.

In the dim light they could make out that the cabin was divided into cubbyholes. Mouldy wooden partitions and boards still stood half upright.

'This must be where the pirates slept,' said Marinka.

'Pirates?'

'Of course. With red beards and a patch over one eye. They each had to have a cubbyhole for their treasure.'

'Rubbish,' declared Podgy.

'Suppose the pirates are on the island now?' cried Marinka. Her eyes sparkled. 'Living at the back of the mountain. And they've caught Gus.'

'Do you think that's it, Captain?' asked Podgy, frowning.

But the Little Captain made no reply. He was looking around very thoughtfully. He had never seen such a strange ship.

'We must go and tell Timid Thomas about the pirates,' said Marinka. 'He'll be pleased to hear that.'

Thomas had stayed on the shore. Not for a whole sack of gold would he have climbed aboard an old wreck like that. He preferred to stay down on the sand and gaze at the wide sea and the foaming waves. If he had looked behind him he would have leapt on board like lightning, but Thomas did not look round. Suddenly a hairy arm gripped him and he gave a yelp of fear. Just one. Because he was hoisted up and carried off so fast that he was struck dumb with fright. Up the hill they went in huge bounds, higher and higher, then down the other side. 'Help!' gasped Thomas, nearly smothered, but the others couldn't hear him.

They only heard his first surprised yelp, and Marinka said: 'Goodness, he's afraid already, and we haven't even told him yet.'

'Thomas is always afraid,' said Podgy. 'Never mind him.'

They searched through the whole ship, but there was no trace of gold or silver or jewels that might have been a king's ransom.

'It isn't a pirate ship,' said the Little Captain. 'But it isn't an ordinary ship either. It's a spooky sort of ship.'

They climbed up the steps again, and each step groaned like a ghost. The door rattled in the wind and the deck was as slippery and slimy as an eel. Podgy slipped and banged his head against the rail.

'Ow!' he yelled. 'Hey! Where's Thomas?'

'Run away, of course,' said Marinka.

The Little Captain ran up the beach. He looked, and looked again, and then he gave a shout.

Marinka and Podgy ran to him and looked at the ground where he was pointing.

There were tracks in the sand.

'Thomas's?' asked Podgy. 'Was he running on his bare feet?'

'Don't be such a nitwit. Those aren't bare feet. They're hands,' said Marinka. 'Thomas has been standing on his hands.'

'Thomas? Ha ha! And then he went for a walk on them'—Podgy pointed to the tracks—'that way.'

Marinka looked cross, but the Little Captain said nothing. He followed the strange handprints to the foot of the mountain. There they disappeared among the bushes and rocks and stones.

'What could have happened?' asked Marinka, turning rather pale.

'Perhaps it was someone with big gloves on his feet,' said Podgy.

The Little Captain had no answer to the riddle.

'We must follow him!' cried Marinka.

Podgy tried to climb higher, but the hill was far too steep, bristling with boulders, briars and brambles.

'It's horrible here!' cried Marinka, suddenly bursting into tears. 'It's a horrible island, a horrible wreck, and everyone disappears in a horrible way.'

But the Little Captain said: 'We'll go and see what lies behind the mountain.'

'How?' asked Podgy.

'In the *Neversink*,' said the Little Captain. 'We'll sail up the river through the tunnel, and there we'll land and search for Thomas and Gus.'

'Yes,' said Podgy. 'And for the handwalker.'

But would they succeed? Would the brave ship *Neversink* be able to sail against the stream? Or would she founder on the rocks and become a wreck like the CIR...?

Trapped

The Little Captain, Marinka and Podgy ran back to the *Neversink*. They pulled up the anchor, stoked the fire and pushed off. The boat sailed at full speed along the coast towards the place where the river flowed into the sea. The six-bucket funnel belched black clouds of smoke and white puffs of steam and the *Neversink* made such good speed that the rope pulling the raft almost snapped.

The Little Captain stood at the helm, sure and steady, and called: 'Ready?'

'Aye, aye, Captain,' answered Podgy.

'Aye, aye, Captain,' answered Marinka.

With a splendid sweep the ship turned into the river, and began her dangerous voyage to the tunnel in the mountain. Straining and creaking, she ploughed through the waves. Podgy piled coal on the fire until it overflowed and he kept on blowing to make it burn even more fiercely, while Marinka fanned it with a frying-pan. The Little Captain gripped the steering-wheel with all his might to hold the ship to her course.

They had nearly reached the wall of rock. Now they plunged into the dark tunnel, and soon they were through it and out into the light again on the other side of the ring of rock, inside the volcano crater, at the very heart of the mysterious island.

'Oooh!' cried Marinka, because it was so beautiful.

The *Neversink* was sailing over a peaceful lake. On its banks grew stately trees and bushes covered with scarlet flowers, and among them lay grassy glades so green they looked newly painted.

'I don't see any pirates,' said Podgy.

The Little Captain stopped the engine and let the *Neversink* drift in to the shore. 'We mustn't make a sound,' he whispered. 'We must search for Thomas and Gus as silently as we can.'

Quiet as mice they let down the anchor, quiet as mice they made the boat fast, quiet as mice they slipped away among the trees.

The ring of rock circled the whole island, high and steep, and here, within the ring, they were walking through a valley so deep and broad that they might search it for hours without finding anyone.

They didn't dare to shout. Podgy couldn't forget the handprints they had found in the sand, and decided they must belong to some creepy-crawly beast. He wondered what it looked like.

'Pssst!' whispered Marinka. 'Do you see what I see?' She pointed to a tree, but before the Little Captain and Podgy could see for themselves there was a tremendous roar.

'A lion!' yelled Podgy.

'A pirate!' screamed Marinka.

'Run!' commanded the Little Captain.

They ran for the *Neversink*. Something came leaping after them, but they dared not look around.

'Quick!' cried Marinka. There lay the boat, ten paces away. But suddenly Marinka stood stock-still and the Little Captain and Podgy bumped into her. Then they all three stood and stared open-mouthed. A brown bear sat on the deck of the *Neversink*. From the mast hung a hairy ape. The long neck of a giraffe stuck out of the hatch, and an elephant was trying to step onto the raft.

'I'm dreaming!' exclaimed Marinka.

She pinched Podgy on the arm to see if he was dreaming too. But Podgy gave a shout and pointed the way they had come. Chasing after them was a lion! There it came, its great mane standing out all round its fierce face.

'Quick!' called the Little Captain. 'Take to the trees!'

Like monkeys they scrambled up a strong oak, shaking with fright and scraping their knees on its rough bark.

The lion snuffled at the trunk of the oak. Then he went and lay down, curved his tufted tail round him, put his head on his paws, and began to snore.

'And here we stay,' murmured Podgy.

'He must have eaten Thomas,' moaned Marinka.

'And Gus as well,' added Podgy.

'And now he and the other animals are going to stay here and wait for us,' Marinka's voice faltered.

'Until they feel hungry again,' said Podgy. 'Gus must have been quite a mouthful.

The Little Captain said nothing at all. No one said anything. For a whole hour they waited. The animals waited, all except the elephant. It decided that it was too big for the raft and lumbered away among the trees.

'Perhaps we should try singing a lullaby,' suggested Podgy.

'How sweet!' said Marinka with scorn.

'Or we could shout and yell and throw acorns to frighten them away,' went on Podgy.

'Can't you think of anything better than that?' said Marinka.

The Little Captain said nothing.

Then Podgy said: 'I know who's caught Thomas.'

'A pirate walking on his hands?' asked Marinka.

'No,' said Podgy. 'The ape.'

'Why do you think that?' asked Marinka.

'Because apes' feet look like hands. They look as if they've got thumbs on them.'

'That's right!' agreed the Little Captain.

All at once Marinka said: 'And any minute the ape will climb up this tree, and then ...' Her voice died away and she turned even paler.

'Then I'll catch him by his tail,' declared Podgy bravely, but he was pale too.

The Little Captain said nothing, but he was scanning the wood in all directions, as if he were on the crow's nest of his ship. He didn't seem to be afraid at all.

At the foot of the tree the lion yawned.

Just at that very moment they all three saw what looked like a conjuring trick. They couldn't believe their eyes. Someone floated past among the distant trees. No, he wasn't floating, he was riding. He was riding high up on the back of an elephant. Marinka gave a squeal—it was Thomas!

The Lion-Tamer

From the middle of the oak tree on the mysterious island came a scream. Three screams, in fact, all at the same time. But the rider on the elephant did not hear them, and disappeared into the distance among the trees.

'Th-that was Thomas,' stuttered Podgy, and the branch he was sitting on seemed to stutter too, it shook so much.

'O-on an elephant's back,' stammered Marinka. 'It's impossible.'

The children stared at one another wide-eyed. Then they looked at the lion that was still lying at the foot of the tree, and at the animals on the *Neversink* moored by the shore of the lake.

The wind sang in the branches, the birds chirped and the streams of the forest babbled on.

'Why didn't he hear us shouting?' asked Podgy.

'He could have come and rescued us,' said Marinka.

'Timid Thomas? He wouldn't dare.'

'He dared to ride on the back of an elephant.'

All this time the Little Captain was thinking deeply, his brow furrowed under his big cap. He was thinking about the island, that was really a mountain in the middle of the sea—an old volcano, a ring of rock. The Little Captain gazed at his ship. He gazed at the brown bear on the deck, the ape up the mast and the giraffe's neck sticking through the hatch. And he thought about the wreck on the coast.

'That's it.' He nodded. 'Of course. Let's go and see.'

He began to climb down the tree, branch after branch, slithering down the trunk. His trousers turned green with moss as he went.

'There's a good lion,' murmured the Little Captain from a yard above the lion's head. 'Clever lion,' he said as he sprang to the ground right beside its fierce mane.

The lion sat up. He was a head taller than the Little Captain. He yawned a huge yawn, so that you could see his tonsils. The Little Captain swept off his cap and bowed, then laid his head between the lion's jaws, just like a lion-tamer in a circus. There came another scream from the big oak. Podgy and Marinka both thought the Little Captain was going to let the lion eat him. But the Little Captain drew his head out of the lion's jaws and called to them to clap their hands and applaud now, because the lion liked that.

'Do you remember what was written on the chests on the wreck?' he asked.

'CIR,' answered Podgy.

'Yes,' said the Little Captain. 'CIRCUS. That's where the animals come from. They're tame. They can do tricks.'

A few minutes later they were all having a lot of fun on the shore of the lake. Marinka swept through the air on the neck of the giraffe, Podgy danced with the bear, and the Little Captain soon had the lion jumping through a hoop. The ape blew the brass trumpet. *Ta-ran-ta-ra!* And the children sang:

> 'Oh how very afraid we were
> Of lion and ape and gruff brown bear!
> But hurray, they are tame, so we can laugh
> And ride the elephant and giraffe.'

It was just like a real circus. When the animals did their tricks, the children clapped their hands, for that was what the animals were used to. Marinka ran and fetched some lumps of sugar from the *Neversink* because the animals had to be rewarded for their acts.

'You and your pirate ship,' said Podgy to Marinka.

'Well, it looked just like one,' said Marinka.

'No it didn't,' said the Little Captain. 'Pirates sleep in bunks or hammocks, like sailors. But the cabin in the wreck was really a stable. It was a circus boat and it was stranded here in a storm, I suppose. Then the animals ran ashore and lived here.'

'What about their keepers?' asked Marinka.

Yes, where were their keepers, and where was Gus? And where had Thomas gone on the elephant? For answer there came a trumpeting from behind them. There stood the elephant, but there was no Timid Thomas on its back.

'Oh dear!' cried Marinka. 'He must have fallen off, and he's lying somewhere with a broken ankle.'

They set off to look for him, the elephant and the other animals following.

'Thomas! Timid Thomas!' they shouted.

'*Ta-ran-ta-ra!*' played the Little Captain on his trumpet. He had had to wipe the mouthpiece carefully, for the ape had dribbled rather a lot.

They walked over the green, green grass, through the leafy, leafy trees among the bushes with red, red flowers, and the sky was blue, blue, blue.

'I would like to stay here,' said Marinka. Then: 'Hush for a moment!'

In the distance there was a dull rumble.

'Thunder?' asked Podgy.

'Silly! There's not a cloud to be seen.'

The Little Captain looked around. The animals had stopped too. They sniffed the air uneasily. But all was quiet and they continued on their way.

'Thomas!' they called. 'Thomas! Where are you?'

They came to a clump of tall, slender trees with smooth, bare trunks, and branches only at the very top.

'Thomas!' they called.

'*Ta-ran-ta-ra!*' sounded the trumpet.

And then they heard an answer. A tiny, trembly answer.

'Help!'

'Where are you?'

'Here!'

'Where's here?'

'Up here!'

The voice came from above. There, high in one of the tall trees, so tall it seemed to be touching the sky, hung Timid Thomas. He was clinging to a branch, like a wet dish-rag on a kitchen rail.

'Help!' cried Thomas. 'I can't get down.'

Where Are the Lost Sailors?

Thomas was hanging twenty feet above the ground.

'How did you get up there?' called Podgy. 'Did you climb up all by yourself?'

'Help!' cried Thomas.

'Just slide down the trunk to the ground!' called Marinka.

'I don't dare,' moaned Thomas. 'It's too scratchy.'

'We'll put a bit of sticking-plaster on if you scrape your poor knees,' Marinka said gently.

But Thomas wouldn't come down. He just hung there miserably. Then the Little Captain snapped his fingers. The giraffe moved forward and stretched its neck towards Thomas.

'Come down, Thomas!' called the children, but the giraffe's neck was not long enough.

'Make a jump for it!' shouted Podgy, but Thomas was too afraid.

Then the ape sprang up the tree. Before they could count to three he had climbed it, picked up Thomas like a parcel, tucked him under his arm and climbed back down with him.

'So here you are,' said Marinka, 'and now I want to know where you've been all this time.'

'Oh,' said Thomas, brave all at once, 'I've been playing with the wild animals. Riding on the elephant's back and so forth.' He spoke airily, as if he did that every day.

'So what!' said Marinka. 'So have we!'

'Yes,' retorted Thomas. 'I had just tamed them.'

'Fibber!' cried Podgy. 'The animals were tamed long ago. They're from a circus.'

'C-cir-cus?' stammered Thomas.

'Yes,' said the Little Captain. 'They're from a circus boat that was washed up on the shore. The ape that ran off with you was happy to see people again.'

'That's right,' said Marinka. 'He was even glad to see a fraidycat like you.'

'Oh,' said Thomas.

'But how did you get to the top of that tree?' asked Podgy.

Thomas began to stutter: 'Well ... oh ... the elephant. I was riding on his back and then ...'

'We saw that,' said Marinka. 'And then?'

'Then he lifted me up with his trunk and tossed me into the branches.'

'Did you say something unkind to him?' asked Marinka.

'Had you tickled his ear?' asked Podgy.

But before Thomas could find an answer, they heard another rumble in the distance, the same sort of rumble they had heard before.

69

The sky was still blue, the sun shone, the flowers bloomed, but the birds had stopped singing. Everything was ominously still. ... The ape, the bear, the lion, the giraffe and the elephant lifted their heads and sniffed the air.

Their tails swung from side to side restlessly.

'What is that noise?' asked Marinka.

'We mustn't stay here too long,' said the Little Captain. 'Do you know where Gus the sailor is, Thomas?' he asked.

Thomas shook his head. 'I haven't seen him at all.'

He was trembling a little bit again, for he was afraid of thunder, especially if it wasn't really thunder.

'We must have a quick search farther on,' said the Little Captain.

'Perhaps he's back at the shore again,' suggested Podgy.

'Oh dear,' said Marinka, 'and then he'll see that the *Neversink* isn't there.'

All four of them stopped.

'How stupid!' said the Little Captain. 'How stupid that we didn't think of that before!'

They turned back.

'But we don't know for sure,' said Podgy.

The sun was beginning to set beyond the ring of rock in the west, and the sky was already glowing pink.

'We'll go on searching and blowing the trumpet for a little while yet, then we'll go back to the *Neversink* for the night.'

'We might as well ride,' said Marinka.

She told the elephant to lift her up on its back. Podgy climbed on the bear's back and Thomas clung to the ape, while the Little Captain sat on the neck of the giraffe, held on to its horns with his hands as if it were the wheel of a ship. Then, leaning out, he put his brass trumpet to his lips.

'You lead the way, Captain,' called Marinka. 'You can see farthest.'

So they travelled on through the valley in the middle of the mysterious island. They looked to the right, they looked to the left, they looked all around. The trumpet trumpeted, and so did the elephant; the lion roared, and so did the bear. The giraffe and the ape didn't make any sound, but Marinka, Podgy and Thomas all shouted: 'Gus! Come out, wherever you are. Gus! Come out, wherever you are!'

But they heard nothing, they saw nothing, and all the while it was growing darker. The Little Captain turned the giraffe in the direction of the *Neversink*. He could see the water glimmering in the distance.

They were nearly there.

Podgy gave a shout. 'I see a star already!'

'How can that be?' cried Marinka. 'Where is it?'

Podgy pointed.

'It can't be a star so low down,' said Marinka.

The Little Captain called a halt. 'It isn't a star,' he said. 'It's a light, in the mountains.'

'It's Gus!' cried the children.

A moment later the earth shook, not with the strange rumble, but with twenty hooves and feet drumming over the ground. The animals, carrying the children, galloped up the hill, which luckily was not so steep there. The tiny light became a flame, the flame became a fire, a camp-fire.

'Gus!' shouted the children.

They saw someone crouching by the fire. They saw him jump up. And then they saw that it wasn't Gus. It was a stranger, in strange clothes.

The Castaway

'Who's there?' called the stranger in the strange clothes as he sprang to his feet. He looked very big in the light of the camp-fire. And he looked angry. 'Shoo! I've nothing for you to eat!' he shouted, waving his arms. 'Go away! Find your own food. There's nothing for you here. Be off!'

Marinka's elephant turned round. The ape with Thomas took a few steps backwards. The bear carrying Podgy growled softly.

'Get away!' shouted the man.

But the Little Captain spoke from high up on his giraffe. 'We don't need anything to eat, stranger.'

The stranger gave a start. He almost fell over backwards into the fire.

'C-c-can you speak?' he stammered.

'Yes,' called the Little Captain. He slithered down from the giraffe and walked over to the man. 'Are you the animals' keeper?' he asked.

73

The stranger's mouth fell open with surprise. Only now did he see clearly that there were four children sitting on the backs of the animals.

'What, who, how, where do you come from?' he asked hoarsely. He shook his head in a dazed sort of way and sank to his knees. 'People,' he sighed. 'People, after all these years.' He gripped the Little Captain's hand and shook it heartily.

The Little Captain removed his hand as politely as he could from the fierce grasp and asked: 'Are you from the circus?'

The man jumped to his feet again. 'Circus?' he cried. 'Do I look like a clown? Have I changed so much? From a strong able seaman to a circus clown?'

'You're a sailor?' asked Marinka, who had dared to come a bit closer. 'Perhaps you're a pirate?'

The stranger drew himself erect. 'Young lady, I am an honest sailor. My name's Dirk, and a few years ago my ship was lost and—'

'You're a castaway!' cried Podgy. 'Do you know Gus?'

The man sank to the ground again. 'Gus,' he murmured. 'My old mate ... drowned.'

'No, he's not,' the Little Captain assured him. 'He's somewhere on this island. We're searching for him. Haven't you seen him?'

Dirk sat up. 'You're not trying to make a fool of an honest seaman?' he asked suspiciously.

The Little Captain put his hand on his heart. 'I too

74

am an honest seaman,' he declared. 'I don't try to fool people. We are sailing on the *Neversink*. When we reached the island of Evertaller we found Gus and rescued him. Then we all landed here to look for fresh water, but Gus disappeared. And now we've found you, another of Salty's castaway mates.'

Dirk stood as still as a snowman. 'I don't know whether to laugh or cry,' he murmured to himself.

'Don't do either,' said the Little Captain. 'Help us to search tomorrow as soon as day breaks.'

'Perhaps he'll come here tonight if he sees the fire,' said Podgy. 'Let's pile it high with wood.'

That's what they did. Later, even Thomas was brave enough to come and sit beside it, while Dirk told them about the shipwreck, about the raging storm: how he had hung on to a plank of wood, and how he had been swept ashore, and then felt himself lifted up by a pair of strong arms. 'I thought some man was rescuing me,' he said, 'but it was the ape. I've never set eyes on a human being here, only the circus animals.'

'Did you teach the lion to jump through a hoop?' asked Marinka.

'Every day I've made them do their tricks. I was afraid they'd turn wild again if I didn't exercise them.'

Thomas gulped nervously

'We thought at first that it was the wreck of a pirate ship,' said Marinka. 'But where can they be? The sailors from the circus ship, I mean.'

'Sailors!' Dirk spoke with angry scorn. 'Dirty, rotten rats, that's what they were. Low-down landlubbers! They got the fright of their lives, of course, and took to the lifeboats. But to abandon ship, like that, animals and all—no sailor would do that!'

The fire burned brighter and brighter, but still there was no sign of Gus. One by one, the children fell asleep. In the middle of the night they were suddenly awakened. It was that rumbling in the mountain again, but not distant now. Thomas started up in fear. 'It's right here under the ground,' he squeaked. 'I can hear it. It's right under my ear.'

The animals, sleeping near by, stirred restlessly; the bear growled and the ape whined softly.

'What on earth can it be?' wondered Marinka.

'Gnomes, maybe,' said Podgy.

'Don't joke too much, young fellow,' said Dirk. 'I don't trust that rumbling. This mountain's a volcano.'

Thomas's teeth began to chatter, although he was crouching almost on top of the fire. 'But it's dead, isn't it?'

'Yes,' said Dirk. 'But you never know. It could come alive again any time.'

They couldn't sleep the whole night long. But there was no more rumbling. And no Gus.

'He must have gone down to the seashore,' said the Little Captain. 'Let's go back to the *Neversink* and sail through the tunnel. We'll find him all right.'

The sky was growing lighter and they got up. Of course Dirk went along with them. There would be plenty of room for him on the raft. The animals trotted after them.

'What are we going to do with the poor darlings?' asked Marinka.

But nobody answered her, for at that moment the ground beneath their feet began to tremble. There was a tremendous crash of falling rocks, as if a thousand cannonballs had banged into each other.

'Help!' cried Thomas. 'We'll never make it!'

They made a run for the *Neversink*, still safely moored proudly by the shore of the lake. 'Dirk, on the raft,' ordered the Little Captain as the others sprang on board.

But how could they go and leave the animals behind?

The rumble sounded again, and the water of the lake began to bubble strangely.

The Mountain of Fire

The dead volcano was coming back to life. It was as if a thousand miners had suddenly begun to work with pneumatic drills and sledge-hammers and steam-rollers. The earth shook and shuddered and heaved like the waves of the sea. Trees crashed to the ground and in the distance a fountain of hissing steam burst into the air.

'Cast off!' shouted Dirk from the raft.

But the elephant set its foot on the raft and the ape tried to climb over the *Neversink*'s rail. They seemed to be begging 'Please take us with you.'

'There's no room for you!' shouted Dirk. 'Get off!'

'It's not fair!' cried Marinka, weeping.

'They can swim, can't they?' cried Podgy.

'The water's too hot now,' said the Little Captain.

'Help!' squealed Thomas, as the big oak in which the children had sat the day before toppled to the ground with a crash.

'A raft,' muttered the Little Captain. 'Another raft. If only we were as strong as Gus was when he was a giant!'

'The elephant!' exclaimed Marinka, and without another word, she jumped ashore and skimmed like a butterfly across the grass to where the elephant stood. 'Come!' she said. 'Come on!' She tugged at its trunk and pointed to the fallen oak. 'Pick it up!'

Elephants are clever animals and this one knew just what this bossy butterfly meant. It picked up the fallen tree and dragged it to the water. Then it uprooted another tree as if it were a blade of grass.

'Faster!' cried Marinka. By this time she was sitting on the elephant's back and steering it by its ears. 'That one there, and that one!'

'Only nice straight ones!' called Dirk. 'With as few branches as possible.'

With lightning speed the sailor began binding the trees together with ship's rope, hacking off the most trouble-some branches with an axe. The ape kept trying to sit on the trunks as he tied them. 'Get away!' barked Dirk.

Podgy was busy stoking high the fire on the *Neversink*. The Little Captain stood at the helm, ready to set sail instantly. The underground rumble was growing louder all the time. Now they could see three fountains of scalding steam, and in one place rocks were shooting up into the air and tumbling down again some way off like monstrous marbles.

'Fire!' screamed Thomas.

'There's fire in my stove all right,' gasped Podgy.

'No, over there!' yelled Thomas, and white as a ghost he ran to hide in the hold.

There was indeed a glow of flame at the place where the rocks were being flung into the air.

The Little Captain pulled on the steam whistle. 'We have to go.'

The raft was finished at that moment. The elephant stepped on it, and it didn't give way. The brown bear followed, and then the giraffe, which found its sea-legs were not good, and decided to lie down. The lion got on too, and the ape, which had to sit on the elephant's back.

Dirk leaped onto the first raft (the one Gus had made) and made the animals' raft fast to it. At that very instant the *Neversink* set sail at full speed. Luckily she had the current with her. By this time the lake was boiling like a kettle and they could already feel the heat from the underground fire.

'Can we make it?' asked Podgy.

The Little Captain did not answer. He steered into the river. Before them lay the tunnel in the rock, the water rushing through it in torrents. It was running much faster than on the way up, and the Little Captain had to use all his strength to hold the *Neversink* and the two rafts steady.

'Hang on tight,' he warned.

Pitching and tossing, the boat shot between the walls that formed the ring of rock. She got badly scraped but came through. The giraffe had to bend its neck until its head touched the lion's mane.

'The sea!' cried Marinka, who was kneeling in the bows.

The wide sea lay before them, whispering in a friendly fashion as if nothing were amiss. But at that instant, a hundred thunderclaps sounded at once. The whole mountain shook and the roof of the tunnel fell in. A tremendous wave lifted the raft with the five animals, Dirk's raft and the *Neversink* and carried them all out to sea on its crest. Thomas burst out of the hold and ran to the rail to be sick.

Now there was a fierce red glow everywhere and a fearful cloud of steam shot up from the mountain. The lake inside was boiling. The mountain was about to burst. The Little Captain scanned the whole line of the shore. It was deserted. Neither man nor beast—nor sailor—moved on it.

'Oh!' cried Marinka. 'What could have happened to him?'

Only well out to sea would the *Neversink* and the rafts be safe from that eruption, yet the Little Captain turned the wheel and sailed round the island to search for Gus. But on every side the beach was empty. So at last the *Neversink* and her followers made for the open sea at full speed, away from the volcano.

And then it happened. A deafening explosion. A tongue of flame leaped up into the blue sky. Lumps of earth, stones and rocks, whole trees flew through the air and splashed into the sea. A huge chestnut tree landed right beside the *Neversink*, drenching the ship and her crew.

The island had disappeared.

The Little Captain took off his cap. 'Gus,' he murmured sadly.

But Thomas, who was still hanging seedily over the rail, raised his head. 'I-I-I saw him,' he said weakly. 'He's coming.'

Hail and Farewell

What had Timid Thomas seen? Sailor Gus? But where could he have seen him? Where could he have come from?

Podgy was baffled. 'You must be feverish,' he said.

But Thomas was not feverish. He leaned over the rail again and was seasick. The huge waves made by the volcano were too much for him. There was nothing left of the island but a small rock jutting out from the seething, bubbling water.

But practical Marinka pulled Thomas's head up by the hair. 'Stop heaving for a minute,' she said. 'Where did you see Gus?'

Thomas waved a limp hand towards the water.

'I don't see anything,' said Marinka.

'He's coming,' spluttered Thomas. 'At least—'

Marinka screeched.

The Little Captain and Podgy ran to the rail and peered into the depths. Dirk leaned over the edge of his raft. Bubbles appeared, and still more bubbles, and then foam. Then a twig, branches, a whole tree. It was the chestnut tree that had been thrown into the water near the boat. Now it was rising to the surface again. The leaves were still hanging on its branches, but there was something else hanging on them too—a puffing and protesting sailor.

'Now do you see!' cried Thomas. 'You lot never believe me!'

It was indeed Gus, spread out on the drifting tree like a half-drowned cat. Marinka waved an accusing finger at him, 'Well, you certainly gave us a fright,' she scolded. 'Where have you been all this time?'

Gus gasped for breath, then he turned red with rage: 'Well, that's a fine one! Where have you been?'

'We've been searching the whole island for you!' cried Podgy.

'And I,' declared Gus, 'only went up the mountain a little way and came back again. And by then you'd sneaked off boat and all.'

There was a shout from the raft: 'Gus, my old mate!'

'Dirk!' With one bound Gus was on the raft. The two sailors hugged each other. 'Dirk, old comrade, where have you been?'

What a reunion! What a story!

'The tree was my salvation, my young friends,' Gus told them. 'I had just climbed it to see what I could see, when the earth began to tremble.'

'So you took to the air?'

But Gus had just caught sight of the other raft, with the animals, and was dumb with amazement. At last he said: 'What's that? A circus?'

'Yes, it is. The animals were on the island. They came off a wrecked ship, and we've brought them with us.'

'What are you going to do with them?'

Nobody had thought about that, not even the Little Captain.

'We'll have to set them free somewhere,' he said. 'In a jungle.'

'Oh no,' cried Marinka. 'Let's start a circus of our own.'

'And leave me to feed the elephant I suppose,' said Podgy. 'Twenty loaves of bread and a tub of potatoes and a haystack every day. Forget it!'

'I'm not going to live in a circus,' said Timid Thomas. 'I want to go home.'

'Yes,' said the Little Captain. 'We'll all go home. The sailors too, after all these years.'

So the *Neversink* sailed on over the wide sea. On a long rope she towed a raft with two sailors singing sea-shanties, and that raft towed another raft with a lion, an elephant, a brown bear, a giraffe and an ape. They sailed for three days and three nights, till they came to a strange coast where the jungle grew down to the edge of the water. The Little Captain steered his ship in a great curve, so that the rafts were swept near the shore, and the sailors cut the rope of the animals' raft just at the moment when it almost touched land.

'Goodbye, elephant!' called Marinka.

'Goodbye, bear!' called Podgy.

'Goodbye, ape!' called Thomas.

'Goodbye, lion, goodbye, giraffe!' called the Little Captain, and he took off his cap and waved.

One by one, the animals disappeared among the trees. They would live there peacefully for the rest of their lives, in freedom, and soon forget all their tricks. Then Podgy piled coal on the fire under the kettle, until the six-bucket funnel steamed and smoked.

The Little Captain set a course for home, Timid Thomas swabbed the deck and Marinka mixed an outsize bowl of pancake batter. She made a hundred pancakes, for the sailors on the raft kept roaring for more.

And after they had eaten, they roared again, but this time the roar was a song:

> 'Two fine sailormen are we
> Adrift upon the open sea.
> The tide is low, the tide is high,
> And here we drift beneath the sky.'

They sailed for three days, a fourth day, and then Timid Thomas whimpered, 'We're lost. We must be. We should have been home ages before this.'

The Little Captain didn't answer. Steady and sure he stood at the helm, his eyes on the horizon, steering the *Neversink* and its raft clean through the waves. He was remembering what the old salt had said.

The Misty City

The sun had set now, but its copper-red rays still glowed above the horizon, like a hand waving good night to all ships at sea. The Little Captain stood at the helm of his boat and played his trumpet. The brass gleamed red and gold as the merry *Ta-ran-ta-ra-ta-ra!* rang out.

The last rays of sunlight disappeared and clouds of fog came rolling over the sea. 'It's creepy.' Timid Thomas shivered.

The Little Captain went on playing his trumpet because it sounded much nicer than a foghorn.

Podgy curled up like a cat beside the stove and fell asleep. Marinka baked a couple more pancakes for the Little Captain, who was hungry after all that blowing. The two sailors sat on the raft and gossiped, as people always do when children are asleep.

'Dirk, old friend, I can't wait to get ashore,' declared Gus. 'Not a sight of a human being for so long. No pubs, no mouth-organ, no nothing.'

'You don't have to tell me,' sighed Dirk. 'Cosy home, cloth on the table, feet up on another chair, listening

86

to the knitting-needles clicking. What more could you want?'

'Well, a bit of a dance now and then,' added Gus.

'Yes, a bit of a dance now and then,' agreed the other.

The waves lapped against the raft, impossible to see in the pitch darkness.

Ta-ran-ta-ra! called the Little Captain's trumpet, over and over again.

After a while the Little Captain went to rest, and so Thomas had to pull the cord that sounded the foghorn. Otherwise they might collide with another boat. The foghorn was actually the steam whistle, which blew clouds of steam into the fog. The thirteenth time it whistled, Thomas squealed even louder.

'A ghost!' screeched Thomas, pointing through the mist. 'Over there!'

But the sound woke no one else on board the *Neversink*, because they had grown so used to Thomas's frights. Only the two sailors on the raft looked up.

'Jiminy!' gasped Gus.

'Well I never!' breathed Dirk.

'A town!' exclaimed Gus.

'In the sea?' said Dirk doubtfully.

'I don't care a hang,' declared Gus. 'A town is a town. That means land to me. With beer. And a mouth-organ.' He rose to his feet.

'Where are you off to?' asked Dirk.

'There.'

'Swimming?'

'You barmy?' Gus untied the rope holding the raft to the *Neversink*. 'Paddle,' he ordered, 'with your hands.'

'If only they've got a little table there with a cloth on it I'll be happy,' said Dirk again.

The two sailors began to paddle. Soon they were wet up to the elbows, but the city was coming closer. It looked very ghostly. Only a few lights glimmered through the fog, like holes in a white sheet. Mostly the doors and windows were dark so the whole town seemed shrouded in gloom.

'It's a ghost town, if you ask me,' muttered Dirk.

Gus didn't answer. They came close to a broken, crumbly landing-stage, and he jumped out. The wooden planks creaked as if no sailor had stepped on them for years.

'Come on, Dirk. There must be a café somewhere. Then I can have a dance and you can put your feet up.'

Hopefully the two sailors made their way towards the houses. But there was no sign of life so far in the misty city...

Meanwhile, the *Neversink* had sailed on. As suddenly as the misty city had loomed up before Thomas's startled eyes, it had disappeared again. In his fright, Thomas hadn't noticed the raft had gone free. He dutifully carried on blowing his whistle, counting all the time. One, two, three, four, five, pull! The whole night through, he stayed at his post, and there was no answer from another boat, and no collision. Soon after daylight the fog lifted.

'Good work, Thomas,' Marinka praised him the next morning.

'Will you make some pancakes for me?' asked Thomas, pleased. 'I feel quite weak after all that pulling.'

But before the pancakes were ready he had tumbled into his bunk and in a minute was snoring so hard that the portholes rattled.

Podgy appeared from behind the stove, rubbing his eyes and yawning. Then he rubbed them again—and again.

'Captain!' he yelled. 'Captain, where's the raft?'

The Little Captain picked up the towrope and hauled it aboard.

'The knot must have come undone,' decided Podgy.

The Little Captain shook his head. 'They've untied it,' he said. 'Any sailor could see that.'

'Funny,' muttered Podgy.

'Simple,' called Marinka. 'They've gone to have some fun. Want to bet?'

'But where?' wondered Podgy.

Marinka did not know the answer this time.

'Gone off to drink a glass of beer in the middle of the sea, I suppose?' scoffed Podgy.

'We must go and search for them,' announced the Little Captain, 'wherever they've gone, or whatever they've done. I've a feeling they might run into danger.'

So the *Neversink*, sailing for home, had to change course yet again...

Prisoners

They sailed the way they had
come for about two hours
and then Podgy climbed the
mast to see if he could see any sign of the raft with the
two sailors.

'Land ahoy!' he called. 'No, it isn't! Yes, it is! It's a city!
Straight ahead!'

'You'd better go and get your eyes tested,' said Marinka.
'A city in the middle of the sea.'

'On stilts,' insisted Podgy, and he slid down, ran to
the stove and threw another bucket of coal on it. They
sailed nearer and nearer. 'It must have been built by an
oil company,' Marinka declared. 'It must be an oil-rig,
and there will only be a few oil-borers on it.'

The Little Captain said nothing, but steered the
Neversink closer and closer. Meanwhile, the hatch opened
and Thomas appeared. He blinked and rubbed his eyes.
He blinked once more, and exclaimed: 'There it is again—
the ghost city! Now you can see it. Last night I shouted
to all of you, but nobody took any notice.'

And indeed, now they could make out a strange collec-
tion of buildings. Great piles and columns rose high out
of the sea; on top of them huddled a higgledy-piggledy

heap of tumbledown huts and houses and bridges and churches and streets and gates and shops and shacks.

'What did you say about an oil-rig?' Podgy said, grinning at Marinka.

She pretended not to hear him and cried: 'What did I tell you? That's where they are. Gus and Dirk are having fun in the town. Want to bet?'

'Huh!' sniffed Thomas. 'Well, I don't want to go there.'

But the Little Captain steered right up to the rickety landing-stage. Podgy went to the bow of the ship, rope in hand, ready to make the *Neversink* fast. He threw the rope, as he had done before, but this time he missed, because he suddenly saw Gus's raft. 'Jeepers creepers!' he mumbled. 'Marinka was right.'

The landing-stage creaked as the three children sprang onto it. Three children, not four, because of course Timid Thomas did not dare to venture into the ghost city as he called it. He stayed on board the *Neversink* to keep watch.

'If you discover a burglar, just pull on the steam-whistle,' advised Podgy as he followed the others up the crumbling steps.

It was an amazing place, that misty city. Everything was built of wood, of wood from shipwrecks, it seemed. Unpainted, dull and grey. There was not a speck of colour anywhere. No red roofs, nor green shutters, nor blue fences, nor yellow curtains, nor brown doors. Not a flower nor a blade of grass was to be seen. And it was absolutely silent. Not even a sneeze from behind the closed doors.

'Hey!' said Podgy to Marinka. 'What was that you said about having fun? In this place? Some hopes!'

Then they saw some people, dressed in grey, baggy clothes. They all looked rather shifty and suspicious. The people didn't linger in the dull, grey streets. Indeed, when they caught sight of the children, they stared for a moment and then ran away.

'Dirk and Gus certainly won't have much fun here,' Podgy remarked. 'Where do you think they could be, Marinka?'

The children turned a corner. 'What's that?' asked Marinka. 'Let's go and have a look.'

A brightly coloured poster hung on the wall. In this grey place it gleamed like the sun shining between thunderclouds: a picture of a big blonde woman, wearing a red coat with a purple collar, and an orange hat with yellow veiling draped around its brim. In big letters under the picture was written:

To Galatea's finder bold, the reward will be a bag of gold.

'Gee whiz!' breathed Podgy.

'She looks rather mean to me!' snapped Marinka.

But the Little Captain led them on up the street. Narrow lanes, winding alleys and crooked houses, dull and grey. Every so often they saw the red-orange-purple-yellow picture of Galatea, and once in a while they ran into people who stared at them in horror.

'It's because of your green jacket,' said Marinka to Podgy.

'Is that so? And what about your butterfly dress?' he retorted.

Just then they came to a square, and the Little Captain stopped. He took his trumpet, gave it a polish on his sleeve and raised it to his lips. If the two sailors heard *ta-ran-ta-ra!* surely they'd come. But before the Little Captain could play one note, three burly policemen came marching round the corner. They wore black uniforms with black helmets and they were brandishing black truncheons.

'What's the meaning of this?' they barked. 'On the street in coloured clothes? Do you think you can do anything you like here? You just come along with us.'

'Well ... but ...' began Podgy.

But the policemen had each seized one of them by the collar.

'Don't try any funny business.'

A few minutes later they found themselves in the police station. It smelled like an old, wrecked ship.

'We are sailors from abroad,' explained the Little Captain. 'We're searching for two members of our crew.'

'Well, I'll show you where to find them,' growled the sergeant.

'They're a dangerously happy lot,' grunted one of the others, giving the children a horrid stare.

'Down below with them,' ordered the sergeant.

The Little Captain, Marinka and Podgy were shoved down a crumbling staircase, and into a cell. It seemed to be made of rough, splintery wood. As soon as the door swung open they could smell seaweed.

Timid Thomas

While all of this was going on, Timid Thomas was keeping watch aboard the *Neversink*. And as time went by, he grew more and more afraid. The morning passed, and then the afternoon, and still his friends did not come back. The sun set. In the darkness, there was a creak on the landing-stage. That finished Thomas, and he fled to the hold.

'But gosh,' he thought, shuddering, 'this is the very place where burglars will look.' And he rushed out again.

'Where can I go?' he stuttered in panic. 'Into the ghost town? No! Stay here? No!'

There was another creak on the landing-stage. Thomas raced to the rail and jumped. But not into the sea. He landed on the raft.

'What a bit of luck!' thought Thomas. He untied the rope, gripped the supports of the landing-stage and began to pull the raft along. One pillar after another, farther and farther from the boat, which by this time he was sure the burglars must be searching.

So he drifted on, along the edge of the misty city, until he turned a comer and then he felt safer. 'Nobody will find me here,' sighed Thomas, beginning to feel rather brave. He did not know that soon the current would bring him right to the barred windows of the prison...

The wooden door of the cellar had banged shut. The Little Captain, Podgy and Marinka were sitting in the damp blackness.

'What a hard floor,' moaned Podgy. 'And not one chair.'

'I can feel a cushion,' whispered Marinka. 'No, it seems to be a mattress.'

'Hey, yes,' said Podgy, fumbling his way around. 'Here's another. But it's a funny kind of mattress. It's warm and it grunts.'

'Mattress?' asked the Little Captain. 'More like a mate!'

Their eyes were used to the darkness now, and they could see a glimmer of light from the small, barred window high in one wall.

'Jeepers!' exclaimed Marinka.

'Gus and Dirk!' cried Podgy.

'Just so!' declared the Little Captain. 'We've found them after all!'

But the two seamen were sleeping like logs and didn't wake up until noon. Then they yawned and stretched and scratched themselves, and when they saw the children they used strong seamen's language. The children understood it perfectly, although they weren't allowed to use such words at home.

'Have you two been painting the town red?' Podgy asked.

'Ask no questions and you'll be told no lies, nosey,' said Gus.

'That means you have!' cried Marinka.

'Oh sure,' grunted Gus. 'Let me tell you, there isn't even a harmonica in this town. Nothing!'

'There's something wrong here,' sighed Dirk. 'No nice little cloth on the table. All dreary.'

'Dull as a deaf dodo,' groaned Gus.

'Silent as a sandcastle,' moaned Dirk.

'Dangerous too,' declared Gus.

'The people aren't allowed to do anything,' added Dirk.

'They're arrested on the spot!' exclaimed Gus.

'And so were we!' cried Podgy, 'because we're wearing colours.'

'And us,' the sailors told them, 'because we were singing.'

'What?' asked Marinka.

'Just a sailors' song,' said the sailors.

> 'Come and fill my glass, girl,
> Come and dance with me,
> Time is all too short, girl,
> When sailors are home from sea.'

'Be quiet,' said Podgy. 'Let's try to think how we can escape.'

The Little Captain said nothing. They all fell silent for a long time. Then Marinka spoke.

'This city has a secret. Everything is colourless. Everything except the posters of that woman who's dressed like a rainbow. It's something to do with her.'

'What about her?' growled Gus.

'For Galatea's finder bold, the reward will be a bag of gold!' murmured the Little Captain.

'Say that again,' said Dirk.

'That's what's written on the posters,' explained the Little Captain. 'If we can find the rainbow woman, then they'll let us go free.'

'And how would you go about finding her?' demanded Gus.

'We'll see about that tomorrow,' answered the Little Captain and he settled down and went to sleep.

And tomorrow they did see something, through the barred window.

A worried, white face peered through it. A worried boy's face.

'Thomas!' yelled Podgy.

And Thomas it was; chitter-chattering after a long cold night on the raft.

'Darling Thomas,' crooned Marinka.

But the Little Captain whispered 'Sh-h-h!' Then he asked: 'Have you come to save us?'

'Y-yes,' stammered Thomas untruthfully.

'You're a real hero!' cried both the sailors at once. 'You're brave, Thomas!'

Thomas felt a strange feeling in his chest, as if it was

turning hard and strong like a breastplate of shining steel.

'Listen,' whispered the Little Captain, 'if you really want to save us, go back to the *Neversink*, put on one of the grey oilskins, go into the town and ask about the rainbow woman. Who she is and what happened to her.'

'The rainbow woman?' stammered Thomas.

'Yes. And as soon as you've found out, come back and tell us. Quick!'

'But ... but ... all right,' agreed Thomas, for now he was brave Thomas. All at once he felt utterly, recklessly brave, like a knight in armour.

Brave Thomas pulled himself back to the *Neversink* on the raft, where there was no sign of a burglar, pulled on the big grey oilskins, sprang onto the creaking landing-stage and strode into the misty city. The rescuer of the prisoners was on his way to discover the secret of the rainbow woman.

The Secret
of the Rainbow Woman

Brave Thomas strode into the misty city. He tried to look as brave as possible, and he tried so hard that he began to believe he really was. So, in his grey oilskins, he dared to go up to a grey man in a grey street and ask: 'Please, will you tell me who this rainbow woman is?' He pointed to a poster of the red-orange-purple-yellow woman which was pasted on a wall.

The man actually coloured at the question. His face turned quite red. 'Young rascal!' he cried. 'Get out of my way with your cheeky questions.'

Thomas hurried on, feeling a little less brave. All the houses looked so ghostly, their shutters rattling eerily in the wind. However, he decided to speak to a worried-looking woman, farther up the street. 'Do you know who—?' he began.

'Sh-h-h-h!' she hissed. 'Don't talk about her. If the Grim Ruler hears—'

'W-who is that?' asked Thomas nervously. But the worried-looking woman walked away as quickly as she could.

Thomas walked on feeling less and less brave.

As he turned a corner, past a broken-down, gloomy house, he bumped into a sailor. 'Hallo there, old salt,' Thomas hailed him. 'I'm just off a ship myself. What's all this about the rainbow woman and the Grim—'

'Balderdash!' growled the sailor. 'Why are you worrying about her, you fool? Do you think you'd ever find her?'

'Oh no, no, I d-don't suppose I would,' said Thomas with a shudder.

'Don't stick your nose into grown-up folks' affairs, then. Get back to your deck and swab it!' The sailor swaggered on.

Thomas went on too, not feeling brave any longer. He decided to look for the way back to the *Neversink*. He didn't dare to ask anyone else and when he saw a policeman coming, in a black uniform, with a black helmet and a black truncheon, he pressed himself against the wall. It was actually a wooden door in the wall that Thomas leaned against; it gave way, and he fell head over heels inside. He picked himself up and found that he was in a small garden and above his head hung clothes on a line—coloured clothes, red and purple and orange and yellow!

'My goodness!' called a woman's voice. 'Why, you little noseyparker! What are you doing here?'

'I fell,' stammered Thomas, scrambling to his feet. The woman looked angrier than she really was. 'Cross your heart you'll never tell!' she cried.

'Tell what?' asked Thomas.

'What you've seen in my garden.' She pointed to the washing. 'The colours aren't allowed.'

'Oh!' breathed Thomas, in awe. 'Are you the rainbow woman then?'

'Galatea?' cried the woman surprised. 'Am I Galatea? Don't I just look it!'

'But who is she then?' asked Thomas, disappointed.

The woman took Thomas into her house. She gave him coffee (grey) and a biscuit (also grey) and she told him all about Galatea and the misty city. It was drizzling a bit when Thomas came outside again. He looked cautiously around.

'Think well about it,' warned the woman once more. 'If your friends are summoned to appear before the Grim Ruler, they have to nod their heads to every word he says. They must say yes to everything. That's the sort of people he likes—yes-men. Then perhaps in two or three years he'll set them free. Otherwise ...'

Thomas crept back to the landing-stage. He felt like sailing away in the *Neversink*, but he couldn't do that on his own. He sprang onto the raft and pulled himself along pillar by pillar to the barred window of the prison.

Luckily the tide was just the right height.

'Hallo!' called Thomas through the bars. 'Are you there?'

'No!' snapped Marinka. 'We've escaped.'

'Not really,' said Podgy. His round face appeared at the window.

'Do you know all about her now?'

Thomas nodded and began to tell them about the nice woman with the coloured washing.

'Go on. Tell us everything. There's not much time,' cried the Little Captain. 'They've taken Gus and Dirk away already.'

'Oh dear!' said Thomas, and he babbled on, 'There's a Grim Ruler here. A terrible man. That's why everything's so grim and grey. He doesn't allow anything—anything at all. He's in a bad temper the whole day. And gloomy. A real misery! And the whole city must be gloomy along with him. That's why he's made it the way it is, with no colour anywhere.'

'Why?' asked Marinka.

'Because he can't find the wife he's looking for any-where.'

'Has she run away?' asked Marinka.

'No!' explained Thomas impatiently. 'She's never been here. He's never seen her.'

'What!'

'Only a picture of her! And he fell in love with her picture. And now he wants her himself!'

'Then why doesn't he go and look for her?' asked Podgy.

'He did. All over the world. He didn't find her. And then he didn't want to live happily any more anywhere. And that's how the misty city came about.'

The Little Captain asked: 'Are you sure it's the woman on the posters he wants?'

'Yes,' declared Thomas. 'She's called Galatea. And the posters are the only things that are allowed to be coloured.'

'Very well,' nodded the Little Captain. 'Thanks a lot, Thomas—'

'I've found out more,' Thomas interrupted him, but at that moment the key turned rustily in the door of the cell.

'Quick. Out of sight!' hissed Podgy. 'They've come for us.'

'You must say only yes,' Thomas whispered through the bars. 'Just nod your heads to the Grim Ruler if you want—'

But Thomas saw the door of the cell swing open. He bobbed down out of sight and the heads of the three prisoners disappeared from the window. Thomas was left huddled on the raft wondering anxiously if he would ever see them again.

The Thirteen Candlesticks

The Grim Ruler of the misty city sat grimly on his gloomy throne.

'Open the curtain!' he thundered.

The servants who had to stand by the door as straight as tapers, the whole day long, at once cried, 'Yes, sir.' They ran to the black curtain, took hold of two black tassels and pulled.

It did not grow any lighter in the room, because there wasn't a window behind the curtain, but a huge painting.

'Candles!' bellowed the Grim Ruler.

'Yes, sir.' The two servants ran to a cupboard and brought out thirteen candlesticks with three candles in each of them. They lit them and began to carry them over to the painting.

'Faster!' screamed the Grim Ruler.

'Yes, sir,' said the two servants, running. But because they moved too quickly the candles were blown out by the breeze they made and the Grim Ruler shouted at them again. They set down eleven candlesticks in front of the painting. The other two they had to hold themselves, one on each side of the picture, stretching their arms as high as they could, so that the light fell on the painting from above.

'Stand still!' commanded the Grim Ruler.

'Yes, sir.'

The Ruler stepped from his gloomy throne and walked ponderously to the middle of the room. There he stopped and gazed and gazed at the painting. It was an enormous portrait of an enormously beautiful lady. The artist had had to use seventeen pots of paint to make her so lovely. She was wearing a red coat with a purple collar; and on her head was an orange hat with yellow veiling draped around the brim. The Grim Ruler thought she was the most beautiful woman he had ever seen. He gazed and gazed and gazed and then he murmured brokenly, 'Ga-Ga-Galatea...'

The servants didn't think she was at all lovely, but that was because they could only think of the hot candlegrease dripping down inside their sleeves. 'Oh, Ga-Ga-Galatea,' began the Grim Ruler again. 'Oh, if only you were real, my Ga-Ga— Stand up straight!' He thundered, for one of the servants had moved.

'Yes, sir.'

At that moment the door opened and one of the policemen entered to announce that they were bringing in three prisoners.

'Ah!' cried the Grim Ruler. 'Close the curtain.'

'Yes, sir.' The servants put down their candlesticks, pulled the black tassels to close the curtain and went to stand by the door again. The Grim Ruler took his seat on his throne.

'Enter!' he bellowed.

'Yes, sir.' Two policemen came in, followed by three children and after them still more policemen, all looking very grim indeed.

'Troublemakers!' bellowed the Grim Ruler. 'Rabble-rousers. You thought you could make the whole city turn against me, didn't you? Trying to overthrow me, weren't you?'

'Of course not, sir,' said one of the prisoners. It was Podgy.

'Not, not! Blockhead! There's only one answer here and that is YES, SIR. Understand?'

'You're not in a good temper, are you?' said the next prisoner. That was Marinka.

The Grim Ruler turned purple.

But the last prisoner, the one with the cap on, said: 'We've come to find the two sailors. Will you set them free, please?'

The Grim Ruler turned a deeper purple. 'Throw them into nets!' he roared. 'And dip them in the sea, ten times a day, for ten years.'

'Yes, sir,' said the policemen.

'And after that, bring them before me again,' growled the Grim Ruler.

'Are you going to stay in a temper for ten years?' asked Marinka sweetly.

The policemen tried to seize her, but she sprang out of reach and flitted through the room like a butterfly. She slipped behind the gloomy throne.

'Peep-bo!' she cried, and then she popped behind the black curtain. 'Peep-bo!'

As Marinka touched it, the curtain opened. In all the flurry, a few candles had been blown out, but there was still enough light to see the picture.

'Hey!' cried Podgy. 'It's the rainbow woman again. And isn't she huge!'

Everyone stood like china ornaments. Never before had a stranger seen the Grim Ruler's secret.

But the Grim Ruler was silent. He frowned horribly and his eyes flashed. 'Wait a minute. I have a better punishment! Hard labour! Ha, ha. They can hold all thirteen...' He thundered a command. 'Bring the seamen here!'

And in a few minutes all five were standing in a row before the Grim Ruler—the three children and the two sailors, with their backs to the portrait. They were ordered to hold their arms wide. In each hand was placed a heavy candlestick. That made ten altogether. Because all thirteen candlesticks had to be used, one was placed on the head of each of the children.

'Don't wobble!' screamed the Grim Ruler.

Now the portrait of the beautiful Galatea was lit perfectly.

'For ten years you will stand thus!' shouted the Grim Ruler. 'Day and night! Hard labour!'

Poor Gus and Dirk ... their thoughts were on cafés and armchairs... Poor Marinka and poor Podgy ... they decided they would have been better off in school after all... Poor Little Captain—well, no. The Little Captain, candlestick on his cap, was thinking other thoughts. He was thinking about all the things Thomas had told them about the Grim Ruler. And then he had an idea.

Colour

'Don't wobble!' screamed the Grim Ruler again.

By now the three children and the two sailors had been standing in front of the portrait with the candlesticks on their heads for more than an hour.

The Grim Ruler sat on his throne and he wondered grimly why the beautiful Galatea did not really exist.

'Whoever wobbles, wobbles into the sea,' he threatened.

But the Little Captain did not wobble. He turned round, right round, and looked at the portrait.

The Grim Ruler began to yell some fearful order, but the Little Captain said: 'Yes, it's the same lady all right.'

'Wh-hat! Who?' bellowed the Ruler.

'I thought so right away,' murmured the Little Captain as if speaking to himself. 'It looks exactly like her. He must be a good painter.'

'What are you saying?' The Grim Ruler jumped to his feet.

'And she was so kind to us,' went on the Little Captain. 'What a pity she couldn't find a husband when she wanted so much to be married.'

The Grim Ruler swallowed hard. 'Does she really exist then?' he gasped at last.

'Yes, sir,' was the only answer he got from the Little Captain.

'Oh!' breathed the Grim Ruler. 'Where does she live? Tell me at once! I'm going to find her. Now! Speak up! Where is she?'

'Yes, sir,' said the Little Captain.

'Where?'

'Yes, sir,' said the Little Captain.

'Where, I demand to know?'

'Yes, sir,' said the Little Captain.

The Grim Ruler kicked his gloomy throne into a comer of the room.

'Yes, sir,' said the Little Captain. 'I thought that was the only answer we were allowed to give.'

'But not now!' raged the Ruler.

'Oh, I'm not sure if I feel like saying anything else. You're not being very nice to us. If Galatea saw—'

The Grim Ruler fell to his knees. Then he jumped to his feet again and bellowed orders to the two footmen at the door, and in next to no time the children and the sailors were sitting comfortably on soft silk cushions, at a table laden with cakes and candy and lollipops and lemonade (and beer for the sailors) and toffees and trifles, and ices and mousses (and caviar and cognac and vodka). The Grim Ruler trotted back and forth, waiting on them. 'Have some more whipped cream. Yes, lick your plate if you like. Shall I bring another bottle of wine? Try the coffee cake. Where does she live—do tell me. Another

glass of lemonade? Of course, there's plenty more chocolate pudding. Where does she live?'

At last they sat back, feeling very full of food. A harmonica player was ordered for Gus, and an extra chair for Dirk to rest his feet on. Then the Little Captain said: 'I don't think I'll tell you where Galatea lives after all.'

The Ruler stood as if rooted to the floor.

'Because I've got a better idea,' went on the Little Captain. 'I'll go and bring her to you.'

The Grim Ruler's eyes narrowed to slits. 'Oh yes, you'll go, and you'll never come back.'

'That's not the sort of person I am,' declared the Little Captain. 'But you may keep the two sailors here. I asked you to free them, but let them stay a bit longer.'

'That suits us fine,' chorused Gus and Dirk, in tune with the harmonica.

'As hostages,' finished the Little Captain.

'Hmm,' grunted the Grim Ruler. 'How long will it take?'

'Oh,' said the Little Captain. 'She'll be here by tomorrow.' At that, the Grim Ruler quite forgot to be grim. He danced and galloped round the table, hip-hip-hooraying as he went. And in between hip-hips and hoorays he shouted orders. 'Paint the palace! Paint the city! Every house, every street, every spire! Set all the prisoners free! No, not these two seamen! Hang up lanterns! And decorations! Bells,

112

Drums! Fireworks! A triumphal arch! For Galatea! Colour, colour, colour! It must be like a rainbow for my Galatea! Hurry up! Start painting!'

An hour later, Thomas heard footsteps on the deck of the *Neversink*. His first thought was burglars, but it was the Little Captain, Marinka and Podgy returning.

'Now we can go home, can't we?' said homesick Thomas hopefully.

But the Little Captain said, 'First Galatea,' and the four of them crouched together in the hold to work out his plan.

Nobody from the city bothered to listen to them. No one had time, for everyone was busy with the preparations for the coming of Galatea. With a hundred pots of paint and three hundred brushes, with ladders and planks and ropes, they clattered into the streets. Here and there, low whistling and humming could be heard. Tunes that had almost been forgotten.

Nobody saw a small figure spring from the *Neversink* onto the landing-stage and hurry into the city in the dusk. Like a shadow he slipped through the streets, until he came to a door in a fence, and knocked.

Nobody heard the whispering when he went in and nobody saw him creeping out again with a big package under his arm. Only the two sailors, imprisoned once more in the seaweedy cell, saw through the barred window, an hour later, some lights glide over the sea and disappear into the distance.

'There goes the *Neversink*,' said Gus.

'Shall we ever see them again?' wondered Dirk gloom-ily. 'They've left us stuck in this dump.'

Beautiful Galatea

Dirk's gloomy doubts did not come true. The next morning at sunrise the *Neversink*'s steam whistle sounded a greeting to the misty city. But it wasn't a misty city any longer. On its thousand pillars, in the middle of the sea, it was a festive city with flags flying and balloons blowing in the breeze.

'Hurrah!' cried everyone. 'Hurrah! Here she is!'

The whole population ran out of their houses and thronged to the edge of the sea. The Grim Ruler stood at the very end of the rickety landing-stage. His heart was pounding with excitement, as he peered through a telescope at the approaching boat. But all he could see was the Little Captain, standing at the helm, sure and steady, his eyes on the landing-stage.

'Haven't they been able to find her?' The Grim Ruler turned pale and let his telescope sink to his side. 'Where are the others?' he asked suspiciously, when he saw the Little Captain himself making the boat fast.

115

But the Little Captain gave no answer. He took his brass trumpet and blew. *Ta-ran-ta-ra!* It became a fine tune:

> 'Has she come, will she stay
> Is today the wedding day?
> Has she come, will she stay
> And chase away the gloomygrey?'

With the words of the last line, the hatch of the *Neversink* slowly opened, and up she stepped, the beautiful rainbow woman of the portrait. She was real, after all. She lived and she walked, in her red coat with the purple collar, and her orange hat with the yellow veiling. She was exactly like the portrait, except that she had a veil over her face too. She walked across the deck towards the Grim Ruler.

'Ga-Ga-Galatea ...' stammered the Grim Ruler. He bowed like a servant and reached for her hand. But the Little Captain said quickly, 'No, I'll lead her,' and he helped her onto the landing-stage.

'March!' shouted the Grim Ruler to his followers, and the procession started off, like a long ribbon of flowers. Musicians, acrobats, majorettes, drummers, policemen, marines and the Carrier Pigeon Club, all were in it. They danced and they jigged as they hadn't danced and jigged for ten long years.

Galatea followed the procession at a stately pace. She seemed to be a little unsteady on her feet, probably because of the sea voyage.

'Ga-Ga-Galatea ...' gasped the Grim Ruler. Like a faithful dog he trotted at her heels. 'Ga-Ga-Ga ...'

But the beautiful Galatea did not look round. She waved cheerfully at all the rejoicing people. 'What a fine city,' she murmured to the Little Captain. 'How colourful! How happy! What—ow! Don't squeeze so hard!'

'I beg your pardon,' said the Little Captain politely.

'I was speaking to myself,' answered Galatea.

Soon they reached the palace, where the Grim Ruler had ordered a table as long as a street to be laid.

'Be seated!' he bellowed and everyone rushed to take a chair. Gus and Dirk were there. They and the Little Captain sat at one side of Galatea, with three empty chairs (for indeed, where were Marinka, Timid Thomas and Podgy Plum?) next to them and on her other side sat the Grim Ruler.

'Let us begin!' he roared, and they all chose their favourite dishes.

Galatea ate too. From time to time she gave the Grim Ruler a sidelong glance. 'You have such a beautiful city,' she murmured, 'and so happy! Has it always been like this?'

The Grim Ruler blushed. 'Oh yes,' he mumbled. 'Always.'

'That's a fine story!' The words came from Galatea's middle.

The Grim Ruler blinked. 'What was that?' he asked.

'It's the wine,' replied Galatea hastily. 'They say wine always speaks the truth.'

117

The Grim Ruler blushed still redder. 'But I was so long-ing for you,' he babbled. 'I felt so gloomy without you.'

'Aha!' said Galatea. 'And all the people had to be gloomy along with you?'

The Grim Ruler almost choked. 'I-I'll never do it again. Everyone may be merry and happy from now on.'

'Agreed,' declared Galatea.

'So you will marry me?' demanded the Grim Ruler joyfully.

'Perhaps,' she answered. 'But first you must do what-ever I ask. Let the Little Captain rule the city. After all, he brought us together.'

'Certainly,' agreed the Ruler. 'For you I'll do anything.'

With great rejoicing the Little Captain was set on the newly painted golden throne.

'Shall we lead off the dancing now?' asked the Grim Ruler.

Oh help! No!' came a squeak from Galatea's middle.

The Grim Ruler shot upright in his chair. 'Is it the wine again?' he inquired.

'No, the potatoes,' answered Galatea. I'm afraid I've eaten too many to be able to dance.'

But the Grim Ruler was transformed to a Glad Ruler, and he called 'Music!' pulled Galatea from her chair and swept her round and round the room, until Galatea couldn't go any faster. Still he whirled her round. She stag-gered and swayed and wobbled and suddenly collapsed on the floor in three pieces.

'Dumb-bell!' cried one piece.

'It was your fault!' snapped the next.

'I want to go home,' squeaked the third.

Out of the rainbow heap crawled Podgy Plum, Timid Thomas and Marinka.

A roar of rage from the Grim Ruler drowned the gales of laughter echoing round the room. But still louder was the sound of the Little Captain's trumpet. There he was on the golden throne, little ruler-captain of the once misty city. There was absolute silence.

'Grim Ruler,' declared the Little Captain, 'I command you to leave this city. Go to the mainland and live there for the rest of your life. Citizens,' he went on, 'this is the end of my rule. Choose a Goodhearted Ruler for yourselves, and live happily ever after... That is my wish. Farewell.'

Goodbye for Now

The feast lasted for three days and the people danced until the city shook on its pillars. The Little Captain was made a freeman of the city and was awarded a gold medal because he had been so brave and so clever.

Marinka was awarded a silver medal because she had answered so well as the head of Galatea.

Podgy was awarded a bronze medal because he had managed to dance a few steps with the Grim Ruler.

And Timid Thomas? He had almost given the show away as Galatea's middle, but all the same he was awarded a medal, an iron one, because he had been brave at least for a little while.

The feast ended with a chain-dance through the town. The Little Captain led it, blowing his trumpet, and all the people followed, singing and cheering:

'Hurrah for the *Neversink* and her crew!
They've made our city as good as new.
Three cheers for her captain so small and so clever!
May the misty city be bright for ever!'

And the kind lady with the rainbow-coloured clothes dressed herself as Galatea and led all the people in a dance through the town. At last they came to the landing-stage and stopped, out of breath. A stranger, his head bowed, came up to the kind lady. 'Forgive me,' he begged. 'Please, will you marry me.' It was the Grim Ruler, but he did not look at all grim any longer.

'Will you promise to be good?' asked the new Galatea.

'Yes,' he said. 'I promise.'

Then everyone cried out, 'Then we choose you to be our Goodhearted Ruler.'

There was another feast lasting for three days and this time it was a wedding feast. Gus had found more barrels of beer and mouth-organs than he had ever seen in his whole life and the tables were covered with the prettiest cloths for Dirk to look at. He must have drunk at least a hundred mugs of beer with his feet up on an extra chair.

'Come on, Dirk, it's time we went on to another place,' Gus would say every couple of hours.

On the third day, they rolled into a tiny inn in a side street. It was dimly lit, but when they had ordered their beer and their eyes were used to the dusky light, they both shouted together, 'Max!'

The man at the bar turned pale and then pink with pleasure.

'Gus!' he exclaimed. 'Dirk! My old mates!'

They couldn't speak for joy. They hugged each other and clapped each other on the back.

'So you're alive after all!'

They sang and they drank and they clinked their glasses and they told each other all their adventures from the shipwreck onwards. Max had drifted around on a half-empty water tank, and after a week he had been washed up at the ghost city.

'What about old Salty?' he inquired.

'Alive and well,' Gus and Dirk assured him. 'We're on our way to him now. Will you come with us?'

And all three went off to find the Little Captain.

The next day, they built three rafts: one for Gus, one for Dirk and one for Max. With sturdy ropes the rafts were fastened together and then to the *Neversink*, and so they set sail for home. Every single person in the city came to see them off. With shrill blasts from the steam-whistle, the *Neversink* sailed proudly away the three rafts floating in her wake. A rollicking three-part sea-shanty drifted back over the waves to the misty city.

They sailed day after day on the flat sea.

At night they watched the stars, and the sky was so bright that you could see the Great Bear. The Little Captain played his trumpet and Marinka swore she saw mermaids swimming in the sea.

'Nonsense,' Podgy said, but Timid Thomas believed her.

On the fifth day, he asked 'When will we be home?'

'When the pancakes are finished,' said Marinka, who was mixing up some batter.

'But we're not going home, Thomas. Didn't you know?' said Podgy,

Timid Thomas turned pale.

'Is that true, Little Captain?'

But the Little Captain gave no answer. He stood at the helm, sure and steady, gazing at the horizon as he steered. What was he thinking about? About the old salt, and Gus's story of the *seven* sailors lost when his ship was wrecked? They had found three, and Salty himself made four. Were the other three alive somewhere too?

'Perhaps you will bring all of them back with you,' the old salt had said. Only now did the Little Captain understand what he had meant. The Little Captain had set sail for the island of Evertaller, but who was he bringing back with him? Not all of them...

Would he change course? But where could he find them? For the time being he sailed for home.

THE LITTLE
CAPTAIN AND THE
SEVEN TOWERS

The Storm

On the earth there is more sea than land—look at a map of the world. The sea is big and wide and blue. Or grey, when clouds hang in the sky.

All kinds of ships travel the seas, with their captains and sailors, but there is one boat, a very small one, which has no one but children on board.

The boat is the *Neversink* and she belongs to the Little Captain.

The *Neversink* has an upturned bathtub for a boiler, a stovepipe for a furnace and six bottomless buckets stuck on top of each other for a funnel.

The Little Captain is always steady at the helm, feet apart, eyes fixed on the horizon. Podgy Plum lies in front of the furnace, blowing into the fire. Marinka stands in the galley making pancakes. And Timid Thomas has to swab the deck, because Timid Thomas went along as a reluctant stowaway.

The four children had had plenty of adventures. They had been to the island of Evertaller and grown into outsize people for a whole day. They had been to volcano island, where they had found a troupe of circus animals and to the misty city, where they had tamed the Grim Ruler.

All these stories were told in the first book about the Little Captain, along with the tale of old Salty, who had lost three of his mates when they were swept overboard in a storm, and then suffered shipwreck with three more.

'Perhaps you will bring them all back with you,' Salty had said to the Little Captain before the *Neversink* sailed away. He meant the three mates with whom he had been shipwrecked. He had no hope of seeing the sailors who had been washed overboard again.

And the children had indeed found sailor Gus on the island of Evertaller, sailor Dirk on the volcano island and sailor Max in the misty city. Salty's three shipwrecked mates, big, hulking sea-dogs, did not fit into the little boat, so each had his own raft, with a tow-rope made fast to the *Neversink*.

Now they were on their way home, voyaging across the wide ocean, day after day, but their home port still lay a thousand storm waves off.

Night fell again. The Little Captain put his copper trumpet to his mouth and blew, *Ta-ran-ta-ra!* towards the moon. The moon seemed to be made of gleaming copper too, but its light was suddenly dimmed as a cloud drifted across it.

'There's a storm coming,' said the Little Captain. 'Blow up the fire.'

Podgy Plum began to blow into the stovepipe at once, until the six-bucket funnel belched out black smoke-clouds. The brave little boat ploughed faster through the waves, but the wind rose and blew it back again just as hard.

'We'll never get home again!' whimpered Timid Thomas.

'Great!' laughed Marinka. 'We shan't have to go back to school!'

The wind began to groan and howl and bellow and at last scream. The waves grew into mounds, hills, mountains and finally foam-spouting volcanoes.

'We're going down!' screeched Timid Thomas and he jumped through the hatch into the hold.

'Afraid you'll get your feet wet?' Marinka shrieked after him.

Podgy Plum was crimson from blowing, but the Little Captain stood at the helm, feet apart, peering through the crests of foam.

The *Neversink* could weather a storm, even if she pitched higher than the clouds, but the three rafts she towed were a different matter—

'Another knot in the tow-rope!' ordered the Little Captain. 'With a double loop.'

Podgy Plum stopped blowing—it was not necessary in any case, because the wind was blowing quite hard enough already. He began to haul on the tow-rope and made two knots in it, with three loops.

'Help at the helm!' thundered the Little Captain.

Podgy Plum and Marinka each grasped a spoke of the wheel, but at every wave they were flung to and fro like puppets. And every wave spouted water over the deck as if a hundred firemen were spraying their hoses at once.

'Get Timid Thomas to bail!' thundered the Little Captain.

Timid Thomas, pale as death, was hauled out of the hold and given a bailer. But for every bowl of water he threw overboard the sea poured in ten more.

'We're sinking!' he howled.

It was the worst storm the *Neversink* had ever known. The water had reached the bottom of the stovepipe, but the fire was not yet hissing.

Then came a terrible crack and a shock shuddered through the little boat.

Timid Thomas let the bailer blow away.

'What was that?!' said Plum and Marinka together.

But the Little Captain stood steady at the helm, feet apart, eyes boring into the black and stormy night. Because the *Neversink* was suddenly shooting forward, dancing like a crazy thing across the waves, towards the place where the clouds parted and the evening sun dispersed the storm.

'We are saved,' said Podgy Plum a little later.

But the Little Captain shook his head so that the water spattered from his cap. He walked to the afterdeck and began to haul in the tow-rope. After seven loops he had reached the end. It was all unravelled. Nothing was attached to it, not one of the three rafts—

The sailors had vanished in the storm.

The Whirlpool

'Poor shipwrecked mariners,' said Marinka. 'Now they're shipwrecked again.'

'Yes,' said Podgy Plum. 'And now I can understand that crack we heard last night. It was the tow-rope breaking. That's why we suddenly shot forward so fast, without the rafts and the heavy sailors.'

'They must have drowned in the sea,' moaned Timid Thomas. 'I don't want to stay at sea any more. I want to go home.'

But the Little Captain shook his head. 'They haven't drowned,' he said. 'The rafts were strong and solidly built. They won't sink and they won't overturn. We'll go and look for the sailors.'

'Yes!' shouted Podgy Plum and Marinka. 'We won't leave them in the lurch.'

Timid Thomas began to cry and went blubbering over to the foredeck to stare in the direction of home, but his home was far below the horizon. There was only the sea to be seen, with a thousand crinkling crests which soared and swelled until your stomach heaved. Timid Thomas was seasick.

But the Little Captain went to the helm and turned

the *Neversink* in the direction from which they had come. 'Full steam ahead!' he shouted. 'Stoke the fires!'

Podgy Plum poured a whole bucketful of coal on the fire and began to blow again until white steam hissed from the engine.

Marinka made a fresh batter so that she could bake a stack of pancakes for Gus, Dirk and Max when they were found.

That was why the Little Captain and the three children did not sail back to their home port but went instead in search of the three lost sailors.

'We'll find them soon enough,' thought Podgy as he blew. 'They can't have been driven such a terrible distance.'

'Thomas!' he called. 'Are you still seasick?'

Timid Thomas nodded palely.

'Give me a hand with the blowing then,' said Podgy Plum. 'It's good for the stomach, and I can go up to the lookout for a minute.'

Podgy Plum climbed the mast and looked about him over the blue sea. There was nothing to be seen. Not a dot, not a fleck, not a stick of wood, not even a dead fish.

The waves had calmed down after the storm, but the water was still moving. Moving rather oddly: it was not heaving, it was flowing.

'Little Captain!' shouted Podgy Plum. 'Can you feel it?'

The Little Captain nodded.

'Surely that's not right?' thought Podgy Plum. 'On the open sea—'

The current grew stronger and stronger and the little boat was carried along slowly but surely in a direction in which even the Little Captain had never travelled before.

'Shouldn't we go back?' yelled Podgy Plum.

But the Little Captain shook his head. Hour after hour passed. The *Neversink* was still drifting and Podgy Plum was just going to climb down the mast to have a look at the chart and see where they were heading, when he suddenly gave a yell.

He saw a dot.

He saw three dots.

'Yes!' he shouted. 'There! There they are!'

He pointed into the distance.

'Gus, Dirk and Max! They're standing up, waving their arms!'

'Hurrah!' cried Marinka. 'We have saved them. And there's a stack of pancakes for them, too!'

The Little Captain steered in the direction where Podgy was pointing and slowly the rafts with the sailors on them grew larger and clearer.

But the current in the sea grew stronger too, and Podgy suddenly shouted: 'Hey!'

They all saw it. The three sailors were waving their arms the other way, as if they wanted to push the *Neversink* back instead of calling her closer. And the children could just hear their voices: 'Get away from here! Turn round! Go back! The whirlpool will get you!'

But the Little Captain did not turn round, he steered straight ahead, travelling with the current.

The fire was stoked up still more and Podgy got the tow-rope ready.

Marinka stood in the bows, counting the number of waves between the rafts and the *Neversink*: eighteen, seventeen, sixteen. But soon she was counting seventeen, eighteen, twenty, twenty-three...

'They're getting smaller!' she cried. 'They're going faster!' she shouted. 'We're not catching up with them any more!'

Then Timid Thomas gave a loud yell. For from the distance came a gurgling sound, as of water running down a thousand drains at once, and suddenly the sailors vanished from sight and the rafts and all, right in the middle of the sea.

'The whirlpool! It's caught them!' screeched Thomas. 'Help, help! I don't want to go in!'

But the Little Captain said: 'We can't leave them in the lurch.' And he steered the *Neversink* straight for the spot where the rafts had sunk.

The little boat went faster and faster. It was being pulled along now and the gurgling sounded like thunder.

'Hold tight!' roared the Little Captain.

All at once the whole world began to spin like a top, and everything was green and grey and wet. The *Neversink* was sucked downwards, washed away, like a bit of rubbish down the plughole of a sink.

Down the Drain

Some time later Podgy Plum opened his eyes again. A grey light shone above him and beside him rose a whimper: 'I've been drowned! Oh, oh, I'm completely drowned.' It was Timid Thomas, who lay on the deck with his hair in rats' tails and water pouring out of his trouser legs.

Marinka sat propped against the rail, to which she was still clinging tightly.

'Where are we?' asked Podgy Plum.

But Timid Thomas went on whimpering and Marinka did not stir.

'Little Captain, where are we?' cried Podgy Plum.

The Little Captain stood at the helm, steering as if nothing had happened. 'On an underground river,' he said.

Podgy Plum shot upright, making a sound like a wet flannel being shaken out. He saw a stone to the left, stone to the right, stone above him.

'Where are we sailing, then?' asked Podgy Plum.

The Little Captain pointed to a gateway in the distance. A beautiful light was shining through it.

'What's that?' asked Podgy.

'We'll soon see,' said the Little Captain.

'But what happened?' cried Podgy Plum.

'We've been drowned!' whimpered Timid Thomas. 'All of us! I always said it was going to happen.'

'Rubbish! cried Marinka. She had woken up. 'Little boys who've been drowned don't cry. Here's a new saucepan. Go and bail.'

It grew lighter and lighter. Podgy Plum and Marinka stood on the foredeck, waiting to see what was coming. When the *Neversink* was close to the gateway their mouths fell slowly open and a soft *Ooooh!* came out. But before they could exclaim about the wonders they had seen, darkness suddenly fell.

Something had been moved across the gate, a sort of door made of rubber. The *Neversink* bumped against it, bounced back and lay still.

'Well, well, well, you're in luck!' cried a strange voice.

In the dim light they saw a man. His trousers were made of fish scales, his coat of fish bones and on his head he wore a fish's head for a helmet.

'In luck?' said the Little Captain. 'But we wanted to go through. We are looking for three sailors who were sucked down by the whirlpool. We were too. Have you seen them?'

'Ha ha, the floating sailors? On rafts?'

'Yes!' cried Marinka.

'Down the drain,' said the man. 'Into the sea garden. Lucky for you the plug has been put back.'

'But we want to go through,' said the Little Captain. 'We've got to save them.'

'Save them?' cried the man. 'From the sea garden? Then I suppose you have no idea what sort of garden it is?'

The four children shook their heads.

'Well, then, Ebbmaster will have to tell you,' said the man in the fishbone coat.

He sat down.

'The sea garden,' he began, 'belongs to Father Bluecrab and his daughters and it is fantastically beautiful. Full of coral trees and marine grasses and anemones which need a lot of water. Sea water. So I stand here at the gate and twice a day I pull out the plug. Then all the sea pours into the garden. Well, it doesn't all pour in. It just lets a bit out, the sea does.'

'Ebb!' cried Marinka.

'Aha! Do you people up there call that ebb?' asked Ebbmaster. 'Good, good. In about six hours' time my mate Fludde will begin to pump from the other side. He'll pump all the water out of the garden back into the sea. And it's all this to-ing and fro-ing of water that makes the garden so fantastically beautiful. But ...' Ebbmaster continued, 'not everything in the garden is lovely.'

'What's lovely?' asked Timid Thomas.

'Not everything!' cried Ebbmaster. 'Father Bluecrab is dangerous and his daughters are more dangerous still. They have crabs' claws and they sing.'

'Sing?' asked Marinka.

141

'That's what I said: sing. And fabulously well, too. Whenever sailors are washed down here and hear that singing, they turn all weak and follow it. Into the garden. And they never come back. I think they are bewitched.'

'B-b-bewitched?' cried Timid Thomas, and the rail quivered as he trembled.

But the Little Captain said: 'I'm not afraid of singing. Let us through. We must rescue the sailors before it is too late.'

'Sure you know what you're doing?' said Ebbmaster.

'Take the plug away,' said the Little Captain.

'Not a soul has ever come back!' cried Ebbmaster.

'Take the plug away!' cried the Little Captain again.

He put the *Neversink* into reverse and then steamed full speed ahead, aiming her bows straight for the gate.

'My plug!' shrieked Ebbmaster.

The boat's bowsprit bored into the rubber and sprang back.

Once more the *Neversink* ran in, but this time Ebbmaster quickly took the plug away and, with a hissing and swirling, the boat shot through the gate. Timid Thomas's cry of fear reverberated like a steam whistle under the vault and the next moment the sea garden lay before them in all its dazzling colours.

Father Bluecrab's Garden

Father Bluecrab's sea garden looked wonderful. There were streams and rivulets and pools and moats and ditches, full of blue water, and the banks were snow-white with shells. Sea anemones grew as high as trees there, red, purple and yellow, with green weeds between them. Strange plants for which we have no name hung over the water. There were copses of stalagmite trees and islands covered with twinkling starfish.

But most beautiful of all was the shell palace where Father Bluecrab and his daughters lived. It stood at the bottom of the largest lake, glittering whitely from the depths.

But when the water level fell it stood on dry land and then the mother-of-pearl clam-shell opened like a great gate.

Twice a day this happened, because the water in the sea garden was pumped out twice a day by Mr Fludde and twice a day Ebbmaster let it pour in again. Ebb—flood, ebb—flood, ebb—flood, that had been the way of it, as long as men could remember.

When the *Neversink* sailed into the sea garden the water was beginning to drop again.

Marinka and Podgy Plum did not notice: they were gaping at the colours of the sea garden and all the strange plants which grew there. Even Timid Thomas stood open-mouthed at the railing, his terror forgotten.

But the Little Captain noticed.

'We'll soon be on dry land,' he muttered. 'Then the keel will run aground and we'll be stuck.'

'Podgy Plum!' he shouted. 'Stoke up the fire. We need full steam ahead.'

'Marinka!' he shouted. 'Climb up the mast and see if you can see the sailors.'

'Timid Thomas!' he shouted. 'Get ready to make the tow-rope fast to the rafts.'

But Timid Thomas had stuffed his fingers in his ears so as not to hear the spell-binding song of Bluecrab's daughters.

'Stop it, silly!' Marinka said to him. 'There's no magic, no song and not a daughter in sight.' She stared and stared from the mast of the *Neversink*, but there was not a movement to be seen, not a sound to be heard and nothing gruesome to discover. Just colours and more colours, of strange sea-blooms and sea-plants and sea-trees and snow-white shelly banks and blue, blue water.

The *Neversink* steamed for hours round the mysterious garden and just as the boat reached a large lake Marinka shouted: 'There! There!'

She was pointing to the bank a short distance ahead.

There lay three rafts, with Gus, Dirk and Max sitting on them.

'Hurrah!' cried Marinka.

'Ahoy!' cried Podgy Plum.

'Is it really them?' asked Thomas timidly.

But the Little Captain steered straight for them and tugged at the steam whistle.

It shrilled and echoed between the banks, but at the same time they heard another sound—a scraping sound on the keel, and with a bump the *Neversink* had run aground.

The water had fallen too far. They could no longer reach the three sailors.

'Help!' yelled Thomas.

'*Oof*,' said Podgy Plum.

But Marinka shouted again from the masthead: 'There! There! Look!'

She was pointing in another direction, towards the middle of the lake, and there they saw a dazzling white palace rising from the falling water. The shell palace of Father Bluecrab.

Timid Thomas's mouth fell open and he stopped his ears with his fingers again, because a song was floating from the palace. The bewitching song of Father Bluecrab's daughters:

> 'Warblewind and washing wier,
> White shell shine and fishy beer,
> Come here, come here, come here!'

Suddenly the great mother-of-pearl shell opened like a wide gateway.

'A nonsense song,' said Marinka.

'And they sing flat,' said Podgy Plum.

But the Little Captain pointed to the three sailors and the children watched as Gus, Dirk and Max jumped from their rafts and waded through the water to the pearly gateway.

'Look out!' yelled Marinka.

But the sailors did not hear her.

'Come on!' ordered the Little Captain. 'They are bewitched. We shall have to get them back.' He jumped overboard and Podgy Plum and Marinka followed.

The water had now sunk so far that it came no higher than their knees.

'Hi! Stop!' yelled the children, and splashing and scattering water they raced after the sailors.

But Timid Thomas was afraid. Of jumping into the water with his shoes and socks on, of the enchanted palace of Father Bluecrab and his daughters, and even of standing at the rail.

Timid Thomas crept into the hold.

But he went on watching through a crack in the hull. He saw the three sailors entering the mother-of-pearl shell, followed by the Little Captain and Marinka, with Podgy Plum at her heels.

And then Timid Thomas heard a rumbling crash. The mother-of-pearl clam closed over them like a great mouth and there was silence.

In the Shell Palace

'Gus!' cried the Little Captain.

'Dirk!' cried Marinka.

'Max!' cried Podgy Plum.

Their voices echoed in the cavernous vault of the mother-of-pearl shell, but the three sailors did not look round. They were making for a broad passageway and the children followed.

'Come back!' yelled the Little Captain.

But stronger than his voice resounded the song of 'warblewind and washing wier, come here, come here, come here!'

It sounded blood-curdling, but the Little Captain drew Marinka and Podgy Plum farther into the passageway. They turned a corner, and were just in time to see the three sailors disappearing at the end of the passage through a green curtain of weed.

'Careful!' whispered the Little Captain.

The children crept closer, the song grew louder and at last, scared and curious at the same time, they were peering through a gap into an enormous hall. Its walls were made of shells, its floor of sea foam and its windows of fish scales. In the middle of the hall stood Bluecrab's daughters, all fifteen of them in a row and all fifteen of them singing.

'What grisly girls,' whispered Marinka, because she could see the groping crabs' claws sticking out of the sleeves of their dresses.

'What a dreadful dirge,' whispered Podgy Plum. 'They sound like howling cats.'

But the Little Captain said: 'Look behind them!'

There towered Father Bluecrab, a great monster with upraised hands, but they were pincers, and a forbidding head, but it was a crab's head.

'He's really creepy,' said Podgy Plum.

'Like a squashed ape,' said Marinka.

'Hush,' whispered the Little Captain. 'Listen.'

The three sailors staggered towards the daughters. They did not see the crabs' claws. They did not see Father Bluecrab. They only heard the song and they thought it exquisite.

Suddenly the daughters began to dance in a ring round the sailors. The singing grew wilder, interspersed with shrieks and Gus, Dirk and Max danced with them.

Leaping, hopping, jigging, with a hey-diddle-diddle and a hop-sa-sa, over the snow-white seafoam floor. It looked like a witches' feast.

Father Bluecrab nodded his flat crab's head and shuffled sideways out of the hall.

More and more wildly the sailors reeled round with the daughters and as each one passed the seaweed curtain swung to and fro.

'Psst!' called Marinka. 'Gus! Dirk! Max! Come with us!'

But the sailors did not seem to hear her.

Marinka said: 'Let's leave them. If they want to spend the rest of their lives jigging about with these silly monsters it's up to them.'

'No,' said the Little Captain. 'Because they will drown.'

Marinka and Podgy Plum looked at him in surprise. 'Drown? Why?'

'Well,' said the Little Captain, 'when Ebbmaster takes the plug out again and the sea garden fills with water, this shell palace will be underneath the water.'

Marinka turned pale. 'What must we do?' she asked.

'Save the sailors,' said the Little Captain, 'before it's too late.'

But Podgy Plum said: 'I don't believe it. The daughters would drown too, wouldn't they?'

'No,' said the Little Captain. 'They are not people. They are crabs in disguise. They can live under water.'

Marinka turned still paler. '*Psst! Gus!*' she called again through the weed curtain.

But neither Gus, nor Dirk, nor Max seemed to hear or notice or see anything. They only had eyes for Bluecrab's fifteen daughters.

'They are bewitched,' said the Little Captain, 'by the singing.'

'The sailors?' asked Podgy Plum. 'Then why aren't we?'

'I think,' said the Little Captain, 'that it's because we are children.'

The Little Captain spoke as if he knew what he was talking about. At least, Marinka thought so. 'Then how can we save them?' she asked.

The Little Captain did not answer. He stared through the green weed-curtain at the strange party in the great hall of the shell palace, where the dancing and singing continued without pause.

Time was passing ...

It would not be long before the sea came boiling and foaming in.

Was the Little Captain brooding over a plan?

Deaf Ears

The Little Captain's plan was ready. He felt among the weeds of the curtain and plucked out small pieces of it. He gave two to Marinka, two to Podgy Plum and kept two for himself. Then he whispered something in their ears. They nodded.

The weird party in the shell chamber was at its height and the three sailors were suddenly so tired that they sat down on the floor to get their breath. They sat side by side, with their backs to the weed curtain.

Bluecrab's daughters were singing softly now, something that sounded like a lullaby, as if they wanted to lull the old sea-dogs to sleep.

At that moment the Little Captain pushed his copper trumpet through the curtain and blew. He blew harder than he had ever blown before: *TA-RAN-TA-RA!*

The sound rang through the shell chamber and ripped the lullaby to shreds. The cradle-song became a shriek, all fifteen of Bluecrab's daughters yelled at once and fled from the hall.

'Now!' said the Little Captain.

The three children rushed into the room and before the sailors knew what was happening their ears were stuffed with scraps of weed. They had been made stone deaf: Gus by Marinka, Dirk by Podgy Plum and Max by the Little Captain.

'Who, what, where, how?' blustered the dazed sailors, blinking as if they had just been awakened.

But the children pulled them over by the arms and dragged them through the weed curtain into the passage, round the corner, along the next passage until they were in the mother-of-pearl clam-shell.

But the mother-of-pearl clam-shell was closed. Shut tight.

'What's all this, then?' asked Gus. 'Are we dreaming?' asked Dirk. 'I'm deaf!' cried Max.

And a good thing too. Because suddenly the song of the daughters was heard again, trying to lure the sailors back:

'Warblewind and washing weir,
White shell shine and fishy beer,
Come here, come here, come here!'

The Little Captain battered at the shell wall. Podgy Plum kicked it with his feet, strained at it with his hands and Marinka moaned 'Oh, oh!'

But it was no use. The clam-shell stayed shut, like a gate with three locks and no key.

The sailors began to pick at their ears because they could not understand why they were so deaf, and Marinka had to keep slapping their wrists to bring their hands down again.

'Little Captain!' she cried, 'I can't keep it up!'

And Podgy Plum shouted: 'Too late! Too late!'

For outside they heard the rushing of water. The sea was pouring back into Father Bluecrab's garden. The lake was beginning to fill and the clam-shell palace would soon be lying in its depths again.

The water was already seeping in and the children thought they were lost for sure.

But in fact it was their salvation. Because the water was knocking at the door and the mother-of-pearl clam-shell had been made to open as soon as it got wet. Slowly the two halves gaped apart.

'Quick!' cried the Little Captain.

'Come here!' sang the daughters.

But the deaf sailors could not hear them. They were standing up now, as if frozen ... until their feet got wet. Then they were suddenly wide awake and realized what was happening.

The water was rising rapidly, foaming and swirling. They could see it rolling in through the open shell and without stopping to think for a second the three sailors caught up the three children, put them on their backs and waded out.

'White shell shine and fishy beer,
Come here, come here, come here!'

sang the daughters from the palace.

But however entrancing their voices may have sounded, their magic was balked by the seaweed ear-plugs. Gus, Dirk and Max did not even look round. They sprang splish-splash through the water with the Little Captain, Marinka and Podgy Plum jolting up and down on their backs, to the place where the three rafts lay.

The water was already up to their waists when they reached them. And it was up to their shoulders when at last, pushing the rafts ahead of them, they reached the *Neversink* where she lay bobbing up and down in the middle of the lake.

'That was really mean of you!' piped Timid Thomas through a crack in the hull, 'leaving me in the lurch like that!'

Flight

The three rafts were made fast to the *Neversink* again, the sailors clambered onto them and now it was full steam ahead for the exit from the sea garden.

But the current was against them. And at the end of the lake, on a point of rock, Bluecrab's daughters appeared and began to sing again. And the three sailors began to pluck at their ears to get rid of the tiresome wads of weed.

'Don't do it!' yelled Marinka.

But of course they could not hear her.

'Right about!' cried the Little Captain. He turned the *Neversink's* helm and the boat sailed with her fleet into a side channel, away from the singing.

'We're going the wrong way!' howled Timid Thomas.

He was right there. They could travel faster now, because the current was no longer against them, but they were getting farther and farther away from the exit where Ebbmaster guarded the plug. The channel ended in a little pool with white shell shores and from there they sailed through winding ditches and wriggling rivulets, among waving sea anemones and past harsh coral stumps.

And over and over again there came the sudden sound of the spellbinding song of Bluecrab's daughters.

'I want to go home,' howled Timid Thomas. 'I want my mother!'

But it did not look as if Thomas would be seeing his mother very soon—if at all. They were still sailing steadily away from the exit. And the sailors were still plucking at their ears.

'Little Captain,' asked Podgy Plum, 'what shall we do if Gus ...'

Podgy Plum did not get any further, because at that moment Gus got the wad of weed out of one ear and the first thing he heard was:

'White shell shine and fishy beer,
Come here, come here, come here!'

Like a heavy-eyed sleepwalker, sailor Gus dangled his legs over the side of the raft and shoved himself forward, about to drop into the water. He would certainly have drowned had Marinka not given a loud scream. Podgy Plum pulled the steam whistle and the Little Captain blew on his trumpet.

All this together produced a horrific noise, with Timid Thomas's moans thrown in, so that the sound of the spell was drowned out. Gus scrambled back in amazement and Marinka climbed quickly along the rope to the first raft and stuffed the plug of weed back in Gus's ears.

They steamed on, but when the song rang out again Dirk had just worked one green plug loose and he too was about to let himself slide into the water.

Again the steam whistle shrilled and the trumpet sounded and Marinka was kept busy climbing along the rope. From one raft to another she went, trying to explain to the sailors, but they kept on saying 'Whassat?' and began to get angry.

The Little Captain was worried. He could feel the current flowing faster and faster, and always in the wrong direction. The *Neversink* laboured, the boiler glowed crimson, but at last the current grew so strong that the little boat with the three rafts was being slowly pushed backwards.

'We are lost!' cried Podgy Plum.

Timid Thomas jumped through the hatch into the hold. Perhaps that was a good thing, because if Timid Thomas had seen what happened next he certainly would have fallen overboard from fright.

Snorting and fuming, scarlet with rage, with flapping cheeks and snapping back-shield, Father Bluecrab charged. His hands were pincers, his feet were forks.

'Be warned!' he roared. 'Be warned by me! I'll catch the sailor who tries to flee!'

Even Podgy Plum turned deathly pale, but Marinka shouted: 'He looks just like a broken bicycle.' But she did climb quickly back to the *Neversink*.

The current was so strong now that the boat and the rafts were being pushed back faster than they had ever travelled forwards, but Father Bluecrab was faster still. Wading through the water and waving his pincers he came steadily nearer.

But suddenly there was the rush and swirl of water running out. The backmost raft, carrying Max, the middle one with Dirk and the front raft with Gus and finally the *Neversink* herself were sucked rapidly into a huge, dark tunnel. The sailors yelled, wood splintered, a rattling crash resounded through the tunnel, the *Neversink* bumped into something and there was silence.

Only Timid Thomas's voice rang hollowly from the hold. 'Ow!' whimpered Thomas, 'ow, my head!'

They had landed in Mr Fludde's pump.

Mr Fludde

'Wreckage, wreckage, nothing but wreckage all the time!' said a strange voice.

The Little Captain looked about him. The *Neversink* was lying in a stretch of open water, bobbing against an iron barrier, which she had sailed into. The three rafts and the sailors were nowhere to be seen.

'Ha!' said the voice again. 'There's another bit, I do believe. Out with it!'

A giant of a man appeared. His beard was like a bundle of eels, he was wearing a frogman suit and splashing along in long rubber flippers. Holding a rake as tall as himself he strode into the water and approached the *Neversink*. 'Rotten old rubbish,' he muttered, and lifted his rake.

But the Little Captain stood firm, feet apart, and shouted: 'Stop that! This is my boat.'

'Ha!' cried the man. 'Are there living creatures aboard? Sailors?'

'I am the Little Captain,' said the Little Captain. 'The sailors were on three rafts. Have you seen them?'

'Seen?' asked the man. '*Heard*, you mean. They landed in my pump and now the whole thing is blocked.'

'Oh,' said the Little Captain. 'Are you Mr Fludde?'

'Of course I'm Mr Fludde,' said the man. 'I look after the pump, but I was too late with my strainer.'

The iron barrier was the strainer, which was supposed to catch any floating garbage so that it did not get stuck in the pump. The thing had fallen like a portcullis when the rafts had just slipped through, without the *Neversink*.

'Now I shall have to unscrew the whole pump,' grumbled Mr Fludde. 'That takes hours of work. And everything gets topsy-turvy. Ebb and flood and the whole caboodle.'

Marinka and Podgy Plum, who had recovered from their fright, asked: 'What will you do with the sailors?'

'Throw them back,' said Mr Fludde. 'They'll be returned to the sea garden. For Father Bluecrab. He wants them.'

'You mustn't do that!' cried Marinka. 'The sailors don't taste nice. Gus is salty, Dirk is bitter and Max is sour. They would make Father Bluecrab sick.'

But that didn't matter to Mr Fludde. He lifted his rake again. 'Just let's get rid of this little boat of yours,' he said.

But the Little Captain raised his arms. 'Wait a minute!' he shouted. 'I can think of a better plan. We can help you.'

'Help me?' roared the man. 'Ha ha, what can you do, you little snooper?'

'Listen,' said the Little Captain. 'The pump doesn't have to be taken to bits at all. We're so small that we can get inside. All you have to do is take the strainer away, then we can get through and pull out whatever's blocking it.'

This made Mr Fludde think.

'Sure you're not taking the micky?' he asked.

'No,' said the Little Captain. 'I think the rafts have just stuck across it. That means we can easily get them out.'

'No trouble at all,' cried Podgy Plum.

'Get on with it,' cried Marinka.

'No!' yelled Timid Thomas, sticking his head through the hatch. 'I don't want to go up the spout!'

But Mr Fludde did not hear him, because he was already walking splish-splash across to the iron strainer to lift it up.

Squeaking and rattling, the barrier slid away and the *Neversink* sailed through the opening.

'Where are we going to finish up?' asked Podgy Plum.

They soon saw. There was a room as big as a church and in the middle stood a wheel as high as a tower. There were troughs fixed onto it which scooped up the water as the wheel turned and emptied themselves into the sea above.

'It looks like a fairground wheel,' said Marinka.

'But for giants,' said Podgy Plum.

'I don't want to get in!' cried Timid Thomas. 'I've got a bad head for heights.'

But the Little Captain let the *Neversink* sail slowly towards the lowest trough. Then they saw what had happened. One of the rafts had stuck between the spokes. It had splintered across and the planks were sticking out in all directions like matchsticks.

There was not a sign of the three sailors—

'They must have gone up the spout,' moaned Timid Thomas.

U~p~ the Spout

'Shut up with your whining!' said Marinka to Timid Thomas. 'Do you want to go back to the sea garden with Father Bluecrab and his daughters?'

'No!' shrieked Thomas.

'Give us a hand then,' said Marinka.

They toiled and strained at the wooden planks of the raft which was caught fast in the iron wheel of Mr Fludde's pump.

'One, two, three hup! One, two, three hup!' commanded the Little Captain.

But they could not get the planks to shift.

'Push, Thomas, hup!' cried Podgy Plum, because he thought Timid Thomas was only pretending.

He was right. Thomas did not want to go back to the sea garden, but Thomas did not want to get into the giant wheel either, because it was as high as a tower. If it began to turn again and they were carried up, with the *Neversink* and all...

Timid Thomas looked timidly upwards and then he gave a dreadful shriek. Not because of his fear of heights, but because he had seen something dangling. A sailor's leg, dangling over the edge of one of the troughs.

'There!' screamed Thomas.

The Little Captain, Marinka and Podgy Plum looked up.

'That's Gus,' said Marinka.

'Gus!' bellowed Podgy Plum. Then he asked: 'Why doesn't he look out? Do you think he's still alive?'

But the Little Captain said: 'The sailors can't hear us. They are still deaf because of the weed in their ears.'

Marinka climbed up along the spokes of the iron wheel like a fly. In one trough she found the raft with Gus, alive and unhurt. In the second the raft with Dirk and Max. She tweaked the weed out of their ears and told them what had happened.

'Never!' said the sailors. 'Bewitched? How did that happen?'

They had been scooped up with their rafts, spinning and twirling, by the troughs on the giant wheel, but without Max. He had just had time to leap across to Dirk before his own raft splintered between the spokes.

'Upon my soul,' they said. 'Just in the nick of time.'

They climbed down with Marinka, and their grown-men's strength was enough to move the splintered planks with ease.

'There we are,' said the Little Captain, 'every man to his place again and we'll be off.'

Gus, Dirk and Max climbed back onto their rafts.

Five minutes later Mr Fludde heard a trumpet blast: *Ta-ran-ta-ra!*

He and the Little Captain had agreed that that would mean everything was in order.

Mr Fludde started up the pump. Coughing and spluttering, the giant wheel began to move and the next trough due to rise out of the water would have to carry the *Neversink* along with it. Would it hold? The whole thing wobbled dangerously and Timid Thomas was too frightened even to scream.

Higher and higher they rose, until suddenly they heard a roar like a waterfall. The *Neversink* gave a terrifying lurch, and next moment the little ship was thrown into the sea on a great wave.

'Hurrah!' shouted the sailors.

They were all bobbing safely up and down on their rafts, which had also arrived in good order. The ropes were made fast and then...

'Hey,' murmured the Little Captain, wonderingly.

'Hey!' roared the sailors in rough greeting.

By the exit from the pump stood a post. And on top of the post sat a man, staring out across the sea. He stared and stared until he finally heard the shouts behind him. Then he turned his head.

'Titch!' roared the sailors.

Yes, it was Titch, the first of old Salty's mates to have been washed overboard before the wreck, one of the three he had given up hope of ever seeing alive again.

166

'Max!' he cried. 'I've been on the lookout for a ship for years. And now you suddenly pop up behind me. Where have you sprung from?'

'From Father Bluecrab's sea garden,' they said.

'Bless me!' cried Titch. 'Me too!' And he told them his own story. After he had been swept overboard and counted lost, he, too, had been sucked down by the whirlpool, but he had not noticed any spell-binding singing because his ears had been full of water for three days. And he had been automatically pumped out again by the pump. 'But not a ship has passed to save an honest seaman,' he said.

'Except for the *Neversink*,' cried the sailors.

The Little Captain's gallant boat was already ploughing through the waves. 'Stoke the furnace!' the Little Captain shouted to Podgy Plum.

'Make some pancakes! he shouted to Marinka.

'Swab the decks!' he ordered Timid Thomas.

So the *Neversink* and her train of rafts escaped from the sea garden of Father Bluecrab and his daughters. They sailed quickly away from the dangerous place where the sea poured down Ebbmaster's drain and was pumped back again up Mr Fludde's spout. They were on their way home now, with four rescued sailors in tow.

They sang a jolly sea shanty.

The Lighthouse

The Little Captain stood at the helm, feet apart, eyes on the far horizon. The wide sea lay round about like a giant circle painted blue and his boat seemed to be always in the middle of it. However hard the propeller turned in the water and threw up foam, however hard the six-bucket funnel smoked and hissed, however many waves the prow cut through, the circle around them remained just the same size.

Was there no end to the blue sea?

Podgy Plum puffed his cheeks out fatter still and blew harder into the steam-boiler furnace.

Marinka began on her hundred and twenty-second pancake.

Timid Thomas swabbed the spotless deck for the three hundredth time.

But the home port did not heave into sight.

'Why is it taking so long?' whimpered Timid Thomas. He was missing his school.

The Little Captain did not answer. He simply pointed behind with his thumb. He pointed to the two rafts which the *Neversink* was towing. Towing rafts with four hefty sailors on them is a hard job. That was why the return voyage was taking so long. For the umpteenth time the sun sank like a red football into the water, for the umpteenth time night began.

The Little Captain sailed on, but with one hand he took his copper trumpet, put it to his mouth and blew the seagull song. The four sailors sang it with him:

'How many, many ages long
The gulls have shrieked their seagull song.
They've shrilled their joys and screamed their fears
For years and years and years and years.'

They had barely finished when there really was a cry— from the foredeck, where Timid Thomas was on the lookout for his school.

'A light!' he yelled. 'There!'

A flickering light appeared on the horizon. It blinked.

'On-off-on,' counted the Little Captain. 'That must be the Siliku Lighthouse. That means we are not far from home.'

Podgy Plum had to take the helm, because the Little Captain wanted to look up the lighthouse book. He looked under S: Salamanca, Salzburg, Sarabariboo, ah! Siliku.

'Hm,' muttered the Little Captain. 'The Siliku lighthouse flashes a different signal. Off-on-off... Then what lighthouse is this?' He searched through the whole fat book. Off-off-on. Off-on-off-on. Off-off-off. There was not a single one that blinked on-off-on.

The Little Captain put his hands to his mouth and shouted to the sailors on their rafts: 'Do you know that lighthouse?'

'What?' came sleepy voices. They had to rub their eyes to see.

'Over there!' shouted Podgy Plum.

'The one with the light!' yelled Marinka.

'Off-on-off?' came from the rafts.

'No, on-off-on ...'

There was a strange, confused shouting in the darkness, in which only Timid Thomas did not take part. His frightened face shone palely at each lighthouse signal, for they were quite close to it now.

But suddenly he yelled: 'It's changing all the time! Now it's doing on-off-on-on-off again!'

Timid Thomas's eyes had not deceived him. The lighthouse was blinking all sorts of different signals and the sailors were shouting them out to the Little Captain, but the Little Captain was standing with his back to it in order to shout back more clearly to them, and when he turned round again the light had gone out altogether.

At the same moment a tremendous shock ran through the ship. The keel tore like sandpaper, Timid Thomas fell on his bottom, Marinka's basin of dough fell in splodges and splinters on the floor, Podgy Plum rolled like a barrel into the rail and the *Neversink* was stuck fast on the sand, as solid as a house, or a well-driven pile.

Bump, bump! The rafts, which were still travelling, bumped into the parent ship.

'What's going on now?' roared the sailors. 'Why have you suddenly dropped anchor?'

'We're stuck,' said the Little Captain.

There was silence.

'Then that's a rat of a lighthouse!' shouted the harsh voice of sailor Gus.

'A double-crosser,' said sailor Dirk.

'A wrecker!' Sailor Max had heard about them. 'There's sneak-thieves behind it. Trappers and snatchers. Out for loot.'

'Why don't you just say pirates?' said sailor Titch. 'They'll be coming to board us any minute now. Keep your peckers up!'

Another silence fell.

All that could be heard was the slapping of waves against the bow and the chattering of Timid Thomas's teeth—

The Spiral Staircase

No pirates appeared. No wreckers or sneak-thieves, either. No one, the whole dark night long.

The *Neversink* lay sadly stuck on the sandbank. 'Nice, eh, Thomas?' said Marinka. 'At least you're not sea-sick.'

With terrible slowness the starry sky, like black glass pierced with pin-pricks, edged onwards high above their heads. At last morning broke and the sun banished the clouds.

Some thirty metres ahead of them lay a flat coast, an endless plain of sand, a desert with a few clumps of withered wood here and there and nothing more, no one, not a human being, not a movement, not a house, not a hut.

Except, of course, for the lighthouse.

Like a monster, a monster on its hind legs, a crazily towering travesty of a monster, it reared up out of the flat sand.

Lighthouse?

'There's something up with that thing,' grumbled the sailors. They took off their caps.

'D-do giants live in it?' quavered Timid Thomas.

'Naturally,' said Marinka. 'And they cook like angels. Timid-boy hotpot—that's what they're mad about.'

The four sailors had jumped into the shallow water and were trying to pull the *Neversink* off.

'One, two, three hup! One, two, three hup!' But all their sailors' chanting was in vain. They had to wait for the tide to come in and it would not be turning for about four hours yet.

'Right,' said the Little Captain. 'Then we'll go and look at the lighthouse meanwhile.'

'Whassay? What's the good of that?' asked the sailors.

'To switch the light off,' said the Little Captain. 'It's signalling wrong. There's no one in charge of it, of course. So all the ships will go aground here at night.'

The sailors nodded. 'Off you go,' they said. 'We'll stay here. We've had enough adventures, thank you.'

'I haven't!' cried Podgy Plum. 'I'll go with you!'

Marinka was feeling like a prance on the sand. She jumped onto one of the rafts, because it was too deep for her to wade to the beach.

'Come on!' she called. 'You too, Thomas.'

But Timid Thomas clung to the rail. 'I don't want to!' He still believed a bit in the giants.

But the sailors could not be doing with such a little varmint around their feet. 'Be off with you, namby-pamby!' they shouted. And Timid Thomas was snatched up by his breeks and plonked down on the raft. A violent shove made it impossible for him to return. 'See you later!'

The children paddled with their hands. The sea chuckled amiably. The beach was white and dry and soft. But the wind, the wind moaned eerily through the withered twigs. A witch's wailing.

The rusty door at the foot of the tower was standing ajar. Behind it musty stone stairs, spiral stairs, dizzying stairs, rose far, far into the heights.

'You stay here, Thomas,' said Marinka. 'Then you can warn us if any man-eaters arrive.'

Timid Thomas would just as soon have fallen off the top of the tower. He followed close on the others' heels. Up and up they climbed to the twisting dizzying heights.

'What peculiar bricklayers,' said Podgy Plum. 'Everything's higgledy-piggledy.'

The Little Captain said nothing. He went ahead, groping along the wall in the half darkness. But at first landing a large opening had been made in the wall, for light. The

sun was shining through it and its rays fell on the opposite wall. On letters carved into it. A strange inscription: 'Betelgeuse, Betelgeuse, greatest of all the shining worlds.'

Marinka made a strange sound, but she was not laughing.

Timid Thomas was so quiveringly terrified that he almost fell.

The second landing. Another inscription: 'Antares is turning redder, the Scorpion is a deader.'

'What does that mean?' asked Podgy Plum. 'I really don't think this is a lighthouse.'

The Little Captain said nothing and they climbed silently on. Twiddly-widdly went the stairs, more and more uneven, rougher and rougher, worse and worse laid.

The light at the top was dazzling. A half-open space gave a view of the sea.

'Look there!' said Marinka.

The Little Captain had already seen it. On the stone floor lay the remains of a wood fire. Blackened fragments of wood from the withered thickets in the desert below.

'Lovely lighthouse!' mocked Podgy Plum.

'M-m-m-man-eaters,' stammered Timid Thomas.

They gazed about in silence and in the stillness they all four heard a booming sound echoing from the foot of the tower. The rusty door had been slammed shut...

Then, faintly, they heard the dragging footsteps of someone who was beginning to climb slowly up the stairs.

Even Marinka turned pale.

Could it be one of the sailors?

No. They would have shouted. They would be running up the stairs, they would...

The footsteps came higher and higher. There was nowhere, no cranny where they could hide...

'Woe unto ye, men of the sea!' the voice of the approaching stranger echoed from the stairwell. 'No help can reach you, seven labours will teach you!'

'No!' screeched Timid Thomas. 'No!'

'That rhymes with woe,' Marinka giggled nervously.

The Land of Nonsense and Knowledge

'Woe unto ye, men of the sea!' boomed the voice again, and from the dark stairwell rose a hunched figure—a bent old man, with snow-white hair, swathed in a blue-black cloak, spangled with golden moons and stars.

A magician!

'Eh!' he said. 'Children!'

He shuffled closer, so bent that his hands almost touched the ground, the hump under his cloak was as high as his head.

'Just like a camel,' said Marinka, but Timid Thomas had to fall on his knees.

'Did you make that fire last night?' asked the Little Captain sternly. 'And run us aground?'

The magician lifted his face. His eyes were piercing. 'So, so! The false light, h'm. It lures the able seamen and the boat scrubbers to the Land of Nonsense and Knowledge. You are there now.'

'I want to go home!' whimpered Timid Thomas on his knees. 'I have to go to school.'

A croaking laugh escaped the magician. 'School,' he said. 'We've got something better waiting for you here, sniveller!'

'Ha!' cried Podgy Plum.

'You'll learn Nonsense and Knowledge here. In seven hard labours. When you have finished them, then—'

'Sir,' the Little Captain interrupted him, 'the tide will be coming in very soon. Then we shall get our ship afloat and sail away.'

'Sail away? Oh no! The ruler over wind and waves will keep your ship in thrall until you have completed the last labour.'

The Little Captain looked down over the parapet. In the distance he could see the four sailors toiling on the *Neversink*. The Little Captain felt that there was a hidden power in the magician. The Little Captain realized that he would have to obey.

'Right,' he said. 'We will perform the seven labours. What must we do?'

'Ha, ha, ha!' the hunch-back began to dance hideously. 'Sirius, Antares, Betelgeuse!' he sang croakingly. 'Moon, planet and nebula! I'm coming, coming, closer, closer!'

'I think he's an astrologer,' said Marinka.

'That's it!' cried Podgy Plum. 'And this is not a light-house, it's an observatory. I get it!'

'Without a telescope?' asked Marinka doubtfully.

But the old man himself replied: 'The naked eye!' he cried solemnly. 'The naked eye alone can read the riddles of the firmament, the secrets of the future, the vagaries of fortune.' His own words increased his excitement. 'But I cannot read them! They are too far away! My tower must rise higher, higher, until I can see them!'

The Little Captain pushed back his cap.

'That is nonsense,' he said.

'That's it!' the old man bore down on him. 'Yes, you have said it! And that is your first hard labour. To build my tower higher. Up, up, to rid you of your own conceit. Follow me.'

Like a shambling camel under his wide cloak, the magician turned and climbed down the spiral staircase. The children followed.

Below, hidden behind a sand-dune, lay a great pile of stones. And troughs of cement and trowels.

'Build!' cried the old man urgently. 'Build, build!'

Poor Thomas. He could not carry more than three stones together up the tower. And he would have to carry at least a thousand.

'Gee up!' Marinka was always shouting. 'We shall never be done this way.'

She had to stand with her cheek against the wall and look up to see if the tower was nice and straight.

Podgy Plum laid bricks. Brick after brick. The tower had to be round on the outside with steps inside.

'I'll make it turn the other way for a bit,' he said. 'To get over the dizziness.'

The Little Captain told them what to do.

'Leave a small window here and there, otherwise you won't be able to see.'

They laboured and laid bricks for days and days. They had callouses on their hands, lime on their noses and cement squidging between their toes.

'Higher, higher!' screamed the magician. 'Put all your pride into the tower! That is the hard labour.'

How many stranded seafolk before them had laboured on this tower? Was that why it looked so higgledy-piggledy?

'Slave labour,' said Marinka. 'Poor sailors. I don't trust this camel person. He's just making us work for his own benefit.'

What sort of people were these magicians? Of course there must be others in the desert. The Land of Nonsense and Knowledge, what map did that appear on?

'Seven hard labours,' sighed Podgy Plum. 'What have we got coming next?'

'You're going crooked!' yelled Marinka from below.

Timid Thomas dropped a brick. Helter-skelter, plink-plonk down the spiral staircase.

'They're so heavy!' he howled. 'I can't carry four together.'

But the tower grew and grew.

The four sailors could see it from the *Neversink*. They had long since given up their efforts to pull the boat off the sandbank. They had no idea what was going on. They would have to wait. They were quite comfortable. A hand of cards...

But how many more hands would they play?

Gold-Beating

Timid Thomas dragged the thousandth brick upstairs. The tower was now so high that it swayed in every gust of wind.

'Ay, ay,' said the wizard. He climbed to the top and looked at the stars. 'Look there, the Great Dog Star is awaking in the east. And my comet is rushing away in flames. Westward. The signs are clear! I can read your future, children of the sea. Six hard labours ye must yet fulfil. And the last ... Aah!'

'Have you hurt yourself?' asked Marinka sweetly.

But the wizard swung sharply round. 'Down!' he said sternly. 'Down to the lowly sand beneath and follow the comet. He calls you for the second hard labour.'

The Little Captain took Marinka's hand. 'Come,' he whispered, 'before the tower collapses.'

The twisting staircase was as black as night.

'I want to go back to the *Neversink*,' said Timid Thomas.

'We can't sail,' said the Little Captain. 'The ruler over wind and waves is holding her fast.'

Once outside they followed the direction of the brilliant comet, larger than the largest star: their weary feet trudged through the desert sand.

'I wonder if we shall ever meet a wizard like that again,' said Podgy Plum. 'It's an odd country, this.'

'Very jolly,' said Marinka. 'Don't you think so, Little Captain?'

But the Little Captain took his copper trumpet. The starlight struck sparks from it and he blew a march to keep their spirits up.

> 'One two, one two,
> On land go we, on land go we,
> No more at sea, no more at sea,
> No, no! On land we go!'

Then the sun came up.

'Help!' cried Timid Thomas.

Before them reared a tower which looked rather like a dragon, because red and yellow and green and blue smoke-clouds were constantly belching from it, and flames, too. From top and sides and front and back.

'Do you think they're making fireworks?' asked Podgy Plum.

'Of course not,' said Marinka. 'Cotton reels.'

The door was fire-blackened and looked hot, but the Little Captain pushed it open. The pressure of his hand left a white mark behind. The interior was filled with smoke and stench and iron hammer blows and fire.

'*Atishoo*,' sneezed Marinka.

The iron hammer blows stopped and out of the dancing shadows a dwarf appeared.

A dwarf?

He was bigger than the children, as fat as a barrel and had no neck. And his hands...

Timid Thomas shrank back.

... One hand was an iron hammer, the other an iron hook.

'Ah, the bellows!' said the dwarf in a harsh voice. 'You've come at the right time. The iron is just about ready.'

He poked the children in the back, pushing them towards an anvil where a coal fire glowed. 'Blow!' he ordered.

Timid Thomas blew out his cheeks obediently, but the dwarf pointed to four enormous bellows which had to be pumped up and down.

It was heavy labour.

'Also all for our own good, no doubt,' gasped Marinka.

'Hold your tongue,' ordered the dwarf angrily, and he began to hammer angrily too, so that the sparks leaped.

'Look out for your shirt, Timid Thomas!' Marinka warned him.

> 'Beat, beat the glowing iron.
> Beat the iron,
> Beat it cold,
> Beat the iron into gold!'

The dwarf sang his song to the measure of the hammer blows.

'Gold?' asked Marinka.

'Indeed!' said the dwarf. 'Your second hard labour. Here in the tower of metals: make gold!'

'Hurrah!' cried Podgy Plum.

'Bellows!' snorted the dwarf. 'You're here to make gold, not for yourself, but to cure you of your greed.'

And a hard labour it was, this second one. The whole tower was in use, from top to bottom. They had to pour out hot smelting-crocks, stir glowing metals together until they bubbled and hissed and spluttered, catch sparks in iron nets and spout steam out of boiling pipes.

Podgy Plum grew thin, Marinka's dress got torn, Timid Thomas's tears steamed, but the Little Captain grasped the hammer. He smashed it down on the bar of iron that they had made with so much toil, and he struck so hard that at the ninth stroke it flew into a hundred pieces. A hundred gold pieces.

'Well struck!' cried the dwarf. 'There lies your greed in fragments. Be off to your third labour.'

Marinka tried to snatch up a gold piece from the ground, but the dwarf pushed her roughly out of the door with the others.

'Over there,' he pointed. 'The tower of pots and pans is where you're bidden.'

'Please, sir,' howled Timid Thomas, fawning, 'I'll get into trouble if I come home too late.'

'Get going!' snarled the soot-blackened monstrosity. Timid Thomas got a shove in the back from the hammer-hand.

Off they trudged across the uneven sand.

'I'm hungry,' said Podgy Plum. He sniffed the air. 'I can smell something—'

Far in the distance a tower came into view. A round tower, full of corners and curves and angles.

'Perhaps this is going to be something nice at last!' cried Marinka.

But...

More Hard Labours

'I can't go on,' sighed Timid Thomas. 'Oh dear! Oh dear!'

'And you who were so hungry!' said Marinka.

'Ugh,' said Thomas. 'I'm going to be ug-ug-sick.'

'Eat up,' said Podgy Plum. He was still champing away. There was room in his belly.

The Little Captain took off his cap.

The children were busy with their third hard labour in the Land of Nonsense and Knowledge. They were in the tower of pots and pans, it was the chimney of a cooking oven where an enormous bowl of sloppy gruel stood bubbling. A grizzled cook served them plateful after plateful of the stuff.

'Hup, guzzlers, hup, guzzlers!' he cried, and each time he turned on an enormous cooking timer. 'When that rings, plates must be empty for the next helping.'

'H-how much more?' asked Timid Thomas, retching.

'Until the pilot light goes out,' said the cook. 'That's when your gluttony will be cured.'

'I'm jolly well not going to eat any more,' whimpered Timid Thomas.

'Empty words,' said the grizzled cook, 'and where there's emptiness there's room for gruel.' A ladleful plopped into Thomas's dish.

The Little Captain waved his cap, but not to cool himself. He waved at the pilot light, and—pop! the flame under the pan of simmering gruel went out. 'Where is the fourth hard labour?' he asked.

The grizzled cook had not been watching and looked astounded. 'Faster than I thought,' he grumbled. 'Quick eaters.'

But he still made sure Timid Thomas emptied that last plateful.

After that Timid Thomas had to be carried to the next tower, fortunately not far away. And, finally, Timid Thomas's recumbent figure had to be parked in a hammock, because he was too fat to move himself.

There were other hammocks there, stretched high above the ground between two towers. The fourth hard labour was to lie. To lie in order to be cured of sloth. To lie still for days and days.

At first it was fine. But when, after three days, Podgy Plum simply tried to scratch his head the hammock began to rock so dangerously that he almost fell out. And the ground was a very long way down.

There below stood the great yawner in his nightcap.

'Poltroon!' he roared furiously. 'You're supposed to laze! Until you're nothing but a lolling lummock!'

'Don't bellow like that!' Marinka shouted back angrily. 'You're waking us up.'

After five days it was no longer a joke.

After seven days their backs were curved like bananas.

On the ninth day it was over. They were lowered down and directed to the next tower. Bent as bananas they trudged towards it. The tower was full of screaming and squabbling. There were stone fists sticking out of the walls and inside the children began to quarrel as they bumped into them.

'Leave off!' 'Ooh, you hurt me!' 'Take that!'

'Little Captain, you're an idiot!' cried Podgy Plum. 'It's all your fault.'

They began to fight, Timid Thomas got bruised and scratched, and that was the hard labour in the tower of discord, to teach them kindliness.

With black eyes and covered with bites and bumps and grazes and sores they staggered on through the Land of Nonsense and Knowledge. The Little Captain was limping, Podgy Plum was yelping, Marinka had a cauliflower ear and Timid Thomas had a bloody nose.

Two more hard labours left! Would they hold out? Timid Thomas stopped.

'Come on,' said Marinka. She put her arm round him. 'Come on, Tom, if we help each other we'll make it all right.' She meant it, she was just being kind.

'I'm so frightened,' said Thomas.

'We're with you,' said Podgy Plum. 'And you know, where the Little Captain is nothing can happen to you.'

'Is that true, Little Captain?' asked Thomas. He choked back his tears.

The Little Captain looked at him. He would have said something, but suddenly they heard the pounding of hooves behind them. A horseman was approaching at full gallop. He was wearing a yellow-brown cloak, the colour of the desert sand, and a red cloth over his mouth and nose.

A highwayman.

'Ah, little reptiles!' he shouted in a harsh voice. 'You're all right. You will do. Come with me!'

This was to be the sixth hard labour. The robber led the children to a tower like a fortress. A tower like a bastion. No door, no windows, and hard as concrete.

'In there,' said the highwayman, 'in a dark strong-room, lies the sparkling diamond of bright thoughts. Go and snatch it.'

'That's to cure us of thieving, I suppose?' said Marinka.

'Right!' cried the robber. 'You've already got some knowledge, I see!'

But the Little Captain asked: 'Snatch? How?'

The highwayman pointed to a round opening at the foot of the tower, half buried in the sand.

'Little reptiles can creep through there,' he said.

Timid Thomas fell on his knees to ask if he had to, but he was given a sudden push and slid inside. He slid

The Diamond of Bright Thoughts

The diamond of bright thoughts lay at the top of the tower. Up twelve concrete flights of stairs. There it was guarded by a bullfrog as big as an elephant.

They could climb the twelve flights of stairs all right, but no one could get past the bullfrog. Day and night the creature sat there with its yellow eyes as wide as windows, staring at the diamond. If it even shifted slightly, the brute would start to bellow like a siren and everyone would come running from the farthest corners of the Land of Nonsense and Knowledge.

No thief could hope to escape with the diamond.

If the Little Captain had known all this, he might not have climbed to the top. But the Little Captain did not know, and in the darkness of the cellar in which they had landed he found the stairs.

The four of them climbed upwards, Timid Thomas was last. Step by step, up twelve concrete flights of stairs, and halfway up the twelfth they saw the bullfrog.

'Mother!' Timid Thomas was just about to cry, but the Little Captain clapped his hand over Thomas's mouth just in time. 'Sssh!'

'How are we going to get rid of that creature?' whispered Podgy Plum.

'We'll have to scare it,' Marinka whispered back. 'Disguise yourself as a heron.' For herons eat bullfrogs.

But the Little Captain gave her a nudge to be quiet and crept warily on.

The diamond of bright thoughts shimmered in the feeble light. It shimmered in the Little Captain's eyes and the Little Captain's thoughts grew bright. It shimmered in the bullfrog's eyes, but the bullfrog had no thoughts at all.

So when the Little Captain pulled a brass button off his jacket, polished it till it shone, laid it softly beside the diamond and as softly took the diamond away, the bullfrog found the shimmering button just as bright as the shimmering diamond.

It did not bellow.

But the Little Captain almost gave a scream, because the diamond of bright thoughts was hot (to discourage thieves). You could hardly hold it in your hands.

'Here!' hissed the Little Captain to Podgy Plum. 'Hold tight!'

'Here!' whispered Podgy Plum to Marinka. 'Hold tight!'

'Here!' whispered Marinka to Timid Thomas. 'Hold—'

'*Ow-ow-ow-ow!*' roared Timid Thomas. He dropped the hot diamond on the outspread foot of the bullfrog. It sizzled.

Then the bellowing broke loose. Echoing croaks and groans and trumpetings. Such a fearful din boomed through the tower that the concrete shuddered and shook with it... The secret door at the bottom of the building flew open.

'Quick!' cried the Little Captain. They tore downstairs, passing the hot diamond between them, down twelve flights and through the open door to the outside.

But through the open door the bellowing of the bull-frog also rang out, right across the Land of Nonsense and Knowledge, until everyone came running. The great yawner and the grizzled cook with a rolling-pin, the giant dwarf with his hook and hammer-hand and the astrologer who had cried 'Woe unto ye, men of the sea!'

'Quick!' cried the Little Captain. He snatched the hot diamond and passed it to Podgy Plum, who passed it to Marinka, who passed it to Timid Thomas, and all the time they were rushing on like rugby players across the playing-field.

'Ow, catch! Ow, catch! Ow, catch!' they shouted, and they were getting on nicely when they heard the trampling of hooves. The highwayman was coming after them, faster than all the others, and he was shouting: 'Hand over the diamond!'

He would soon overtake them.

But the diamond gave bright thoughts whenever one of the children caught it. Without even having to speak to one another they formed the same plan.

'Here you are!' the Little Captain shouted to the highwayman, 'catch!' He threw, but the diamond sailed over the highwayman's head and Podgy Plum caught it.

'Here you are!' But again the sparkler shot past the man and Marinka caught it.

'Catch, can't you!' they called. And now they were throwing the diamond so close to the highwayman that he reached out with his hand. Too far. He lost his balance and fell from the saddle.

'Quick!' cried the Little Captain. He jumped onto the horse, Marinka behind him, Podgy Plum behind Marinka and Timid Thomas—

Timid Thomas had to throw the diamond back first, to the Little Captain. He did, but by then the great yawner and the grizzled cook and the iron dwarf were so close that Timid Thomas had no time to jump. He could only grab at the tail of the horse.

'Woe, woe!' cried the astrologer.

But the Little Captain shouted: 'Gee up!' The horse shot forward, and Timid Thomas had to scamper behind, hanging on to its tail.

The iron dwarf's hook hand ripped his shirt, the grizzled cook's rolling-pin struck him on the seat of the pants, but the horse galloped faster, and even the robber, who had scrambled to his feet, could not catch up with it.

This was indeed a hard labour, because Thomas had to pelt along, taking huge strides, and the diamond of bright thoughts burned their hands, however quickly they passed it to one another as they rode.

Moreover, there was still one hard labour ahead of them. The seventh. What awaited them in that tower?

The Seventh Tower

Panting, the children reached the seventh tower. Timid Thomas had no legs left after all that bounding behind the horse, and no hands after all that clinging to the tail. Podgy Plum, Marinka and the Little Captain had no bottoms left after bumpety-thumping along on the horse's back, and no hands because of the hot diamond they were still passing between them.

'I can't go on!' cried all four together.

In answer a sweet voice spoke from the tower: 'To bed, to bed, come to bed!'

'Yes!' they cried. 'Good! Sleep!'

The door to the tower, which looked a little like a lumpy mattress, opened slowly and a strangely dressed lady stepped out.

'Like a dollop of whipped cream,' giggled Marinka.

'What's this?' cried the lady. 'No greeting?'

The Little Captain dropped the diamond of bright thoughts at her feet.

'Ah!' she cried. 'Snaffled and snatched! The youth of today! So young and yet so clever. Well, well, step into the tower of luxury. Your beds are made.' She laughed like a cackling hen.

Even Timid Thomas was too tired to be timid. All he wanted was to lie down and sleep. He was the first in, the others still had to dismount from the horse.

When his cry of terror sounded from the building Marinka said: 'Oh gosh, there must be a mouse under his bed.'

But when they were inside they stood stock-still. The dimly-lighted room was full of beds, yes. But beds without sheets, without blankets, without pillows. Beds without mattresses. In place of mattresses there were nails, sharp end up. Beds of nails, rows and rows of them.

'Yes, yes,' cackled the lady. 'The seventh hard labour is to cure you of luxury. Have a nice lie down!'

'Boo-hoo!' wept Timid Thomas. 'I can never sleep in a strange bed.'

Podgy Plum said: 'But we are not fakirs.'

Marinka felt about with her hand. 'Hedgehog's feathers,' she said.

The Little Captain said nothing. He looked towards a corner of the room which was almost dark. Was someone lying there?

The Little Captain walked along beside the rows of beds and there indeed lay a man, stretched out full length on a bed of nails.

'Doesn't it hurt?' asked the Little Captain.

The other yawned. 'Oh, no. It's more comfortable than your own cot. Have a kip.' He yawned again and turned over.

So very, very, very warily the Little Captain lay down on the next bed, with Marinka next to him, and Podgy Plum next to her. 'It's more comfortable at home,' he said.

But Timid Thomas was still on his feet, whimpering. 'Boo-hoo! And my shirt's torn already.'

No one sympathized and Timid Thomas was so tired that he sank down, whimpering, onto the nails and fell into a log-like sleep.

Now the children had performed their seven hard labours, and the ruler over wind and waves in the Land of Nonsense and Knowledge turned the current of the sea. The Little Captain's boat, the *Neversink*, which had been stuck all this time on a sandbank, floated loose and bobbed along the coast to the place where the seventh tower stood.

'Hey!' shouted the sailors, who had built new rafts from the weathered timber on the beach and were bobbing along behind. 'Look over there!' They put aside their card game and began to shout 'Ahoy'.

But it was not necessary.

The wind got up and drove the sea towards the tower until it splashed inside and drove the cackling lady screeching up the stairs. But the nail beds with the sleeping figures on them floated out.

'Look there!' yelled the sailors. 'The Little Captain!'

They hoisted him aboard, with Podgy Plum and Marinka and Timid Thomas.

'Now we can sail, lads!' they cried gladly. 'Homeward bound.'

But the Little Captain pointed to the water. 'There's another one down there,' he said.

Still asleep on his bed of nails, the dark figure from the seventh tower was floating by in the bright sunlight.

'Fred!' shouted the sailors. 'Fred, old matey!'

Salty's fifth shipwrecked mate looked up grumpily.

'Can't you leave a mate to kip in peace?' he cried indignantly.

'But man! You're saved. We're homeward bound. Back to house and home. Back to our wives and families!'

'Can't a man do that lying down?'

Fred was not to be lured off the nails. He had been lying on them for years. The Land of Nonsense and Knowledge held him fast in its magic power.

'Leave him alone,' said the Little Captain. 'It will all work itself out.'

They tied a rope to Fred's bed and it was towed behind the rest—a raft of nails.

So the *Neversink* sailed on, on its long voyage home.

Podgy Plum blew up the furnace, Marinka baked pancakes, Timid Thomas swabbed the deck.

The Little Captain stood at the helm again, feet apart, eyes on the horizon, to see if the dunes were coming into sight.

Or would the Little Captain go in search of that one long-lost seaman, the sixth and last of old Salty's mates?

The Enchanted Ship

The sun rose over the wide sea and the wide sea lay flat as a mirror, because the wind was still asleep. There was not a ripple or bubble of foam to be seen on the water—wait! There in the middle, the water was curling like a cockatoo's crest and frothing like fizzy lemonade. But that was not the wind, it was a boat: the Little Captain's boat the *Neversink*, on her way home, with five rescued sailors towed on rafts. Gus, Dirk, Max, Titch and Fred. But Fred's raft was a bed of nails and Fred did not want to leave it, he was so comfortable lying there.

The day before, they had sailed past the harbour of Siliku and it would not be long now before the home port hove in sight.

Timid Thomas, who had to swab the deck, was always glancing at the horizon, but when Marinka saw him from the galley she called: 'You're going to be in trouble, Thomas, getting home so late.'

Podgy Plum stoked the fire. He only looked up when the Little Captain shouted in a hoarse voice: 'Land ho!'

And, yes, there lay the dunes of their own shores, and even the piers of the little harbour were in sight.

They rushed to the rail and Timid Thomas dropped his swabber overboard. 'How high the dunes are!' he cried. 'Just look at the tops!'

But those were not the peaks of dunes. They were clouds. Black clouds rushing out from behind the dunes. The wind woke up and its first gust made ripples against the bow. An off-shore current.

Podgy Plum started to blow up the furnace to increase the heat, but the wind grew steadily stronger. However hard the six-bucket funnel rattled, the steam boiler strained and the propeller turned in the water, the wind and current forced the *Neversink* and her heavy tow slowly backwards—the dunes grew smaller and smaller.

'Anchor out!' cried the Little Captain.

There they lay, their home port in sight, forced to wait.

Timid Thomas began to sob, but they gave him a sponge to swab the deck with on his hands and knees.

'It will sink this evening,' said Marinka cheerfully. 'The wind, I mean.' And she went off to bake pancakes.

But when the sun fell the wind grew stronger still.

In the middle of the night Timid Thomas awoke, feeling sick from swinging about in his hammock. He crept up to the deck to hang over the rail, he looked at the foam slapping against the bows, he looked at the distant lights of his village between the dunes and then he saw something which made him completely forget his sickness: a sailing vessel.

A mighty galleon she was, with three masts carrying bellying sails and fluttering flags and pennons. Foaming and splashing she sliced through the waves close by the *Neversink*, and Timid Thomas's mouth fell wide open. This must be an enchanted ship, because there was no one on board—wait a minute, there was a single, lonely figure at the helm, a weather-beaten skipper with white hair streaming in the wind.

'Help!' screeched Timid Thomas, because he thought it was a ghost.

When the others stumbled on deck the enchanted ship had vanished, and no one would have believed Timid Thomas, had the ship not suddenly loomed up again out of the darkness—under full sail, bearing straight down on the *Neversink*.

'Ahoy!' yelled the Little Captain.

'Ship ahoy!' roared the five sailors, who could also see her now.

The enchanted ship grazed their beam as she sped past and above the racket of the wind they heard a hoarse shout. The lonely skipper at the helm had turned his head a little and was shouting something with open mouth:

'Save me!' he seemed to be saying.

'No!' screamed Timid Thomas, diving back into the hold.

But the Little Captain saw the ghostly sails swing across, heard them flapping as the galleon came about and approached for the third time.

'Anchor out!' he shouted, and as the enchanted ship came alongside the Little Captain tossed the anchor over her rail like a grappling iron. It stuck fast at once in the moving ship, the chain pulled tight and they all fell flat from the shock.

The galleon had taken the *Neversink* with her rafts in tow.

But the Little Captain climbed along the chain and boarded the sailing ship. Podgy Plum followed. Even Marinka, her dress flying in the wind, agile as a monkey, climbed from one ship to the other, high above the waves.

Then the sailors climbed along the tow-rope to the *Neversink*, even Fred who was so fond of his bed of nails, and from there to the sailing ship, because they were wild with curiosity.

As one man—because they did think it was all rather creepy—they moved slowly forward over the deserted deck and up to the poop, where the mysterious figure stood at the helm.

The steps creaked under their weight, the wind moaned in the sheets. Was the man a ghost? There he stood, motionless, his hands clamped to the spokes of the great wheel, staring out to sea with mournful eyes.

Then his lips moved again.

'Save me ...' he muttered.

And suddenly the five sailors stood as if glued to the deck. Their mouths fell open and they cried in chorus:

'Hey there, crooked Ben, is it you? Mate, have you lost your bearings?'

The Sad Tale of Crooked Ben

'Hey, crooked Ben!' the five sailors cried again. 'It is you, isn't it?'

The mysterious skipper whom they had found on board the strange galleon clutched the helm still harder, staring at them open-mouthed. Then a faint gleam came into his dull eyes.

'M-m-mates ...' he burst out at last. 'Save me.'

'Save you?' cried Gus. 'What's the point of saving you, man? You're alive, aren't you? We've all been saved, sure as we're standing here. One by one. And you were the last of our shipmates. We have the Little Captain to thank for that. Well, and you've hung on to a fine ship, too!'

But crooked Ben shook his head sorrowfully.

'Isn't she yours, then, this three-master?'

Crooked Ben burst into sobs.

'What are you giving us now? Aren't you happy?'

Crooked Ben wailed: 'Oh, oh, who is going to save me?'

'It's been too much for him,' said Dirk, shaking his head. 'Titch, lad, why don't you take over the helm from him?'

But crooked Ben began to roar savagely. 'No!' he shouted. 'Keep your paws off it!' His eyes shot flame, he looked like a wicked wizard.

The sailors stared at one another.

'He's off his head,' whispered Gus.

The Little Captain had gone down the steps and begun to search about the maindeck. In the grey light of dawn he saw how worn and rotten the planks were. He looked at the broken rail, the ravelled ropes, the wooden barrels and the wooden pulley-blocks. 'This ship is old,' he murmured, 'hundreds of years old.' He looked up at the creaking mast and finally he looked at the peak, to see what flag flew there: a black one, which they had not been able to make out by night—black, with a white skull on it.

'Aha,' murmured the Little Captain.

He returned up the steps to the poop deck.

'Crooked Ben,' he said, 'do you happen to have turned into a pirate?'

'No!' wailed Ben. 'No, it's not true!'

He seemed to jerk at the helm, like a prisoner at his chains.

Marinka had climbed back along the anchor chain to the *Neversink* to bake pancakes. She piled a steaming heap of them on a plate and came back with them. 'There you are,' she said to crooked Ben, holding the dish out to him.

Was the man really not right in the head? Instead of taking a pancake with one hand, he ducked his head like a dog and took one in his teeth.

'Poor soul,' murmured Titch. 'He's lost all his manners, too.'

But crooked Ben cried with his mouth full: 'Ah've bun bewutched.'

'What say?'

Crooked Ben swallowed his mouthful. Then he got it out clearly: 'I've been bewitched.' He went on to tell the whole story, while Marinka fed him like a nurse.

After the storm, which had taken place so many years ago, crooked Ben had floated about alone with the mast until he had been picked up two days later by a sailing ship. 'This very ship,' he said between two gulps. 'Well, yes, picked up,' Ben continued. 'It came right alongside me and I was able to catch hold of a dangling rope.'

To his amazement there seemed to be only one man on board, a man who looked extraordinarily like a fierce olden-day pirate. But crooked Ben was so glad to be saved that he did not ask too many questions.

The pirate refused to bring him into any harbour. Ben had to sail with him to Tangleroot Island. A great treasure lay buried there, the pirate told him, and if Ben helped him he would get half of it.

A strange story, but if you had been rescued from drowning, what could you do? Say yes, of course.

When Tangleroot Island came in sight Ben had to take the wheel because the pirate was going to throw out the anchor. But instead the pirate leaped overboard and waded ashore.

'Bye bye!' he called maliciously, waving to crooked Ben.

Only then did Ben realize he had fallen into a trap. And what a trap! The galleon was bewitched. A curse lay on her, as a punishment for all her piracy. Once anyone had taken the helm he could never let go and must continue to sail the seven seas of the world for ever and ever.

'And since then, lads,' crooked Ben ended his story with a sob, 'I've been sailing and sailing and sailing. Give us another pancake.'

'What about the pirate?' asked Marinka. 'How did he get away?'

'Because,' gulped crooked Ben, 'because I took the helm from him of my own free will. How was I to know?'

Marinka went off to bake another stack of pancakes. Podgy Plum looked thoughtful. The five sailors licked their lips and looked at each other. 'Will you take the wheel from him?' they seemed to be asking each other, but Gus and Dirk and Max and Titch and Fred shook their heads one after the other. Crooked Ben was their mate, but the thought of sailing the seven seas for ever and ever...

The Little Captain was also silent. He scratched his head under his cap and then two lamps seemed to light up in his eyes.

'Listen,' he said to crooked Ben. 'This pirate—is he still on Tangleroot Island d'you think? I've got an idea...'

Tangleroot Island

Crooked Ben looked at the Little Captain with fearful eyes. 'I don't want to go to Tangleroot Island,' he cried. 'I don't want to see the pirate ever again.' And he turned back to the wheel of the enchanted ship, where his seaman's fists were held by magic for good and all.

'You don't have to,' said the Little Captain. 'But I have a plan. Listen.'

The five sailors, Marinka and Podgy Plum leaned forward to listen to the plan which the Little Captain was explaining to crooked Ben. If it worked, not only would crooked Ben be free, but they might be able to take possession of the hidden treasure.

Five minutes later the three children were climbing back along the anchor chain to the *Neversink*. The five sailors remained on board the enchanted ship, which set course under full sail towards Tangleroot Island, towing the *Neversink* with her empty rafts.

'W-what is happening?' asked Timid Thomas, who had just crawled out of the hold.

'We're going to catch a pirate,' cried Marinka.

'A very dangerous one,' said Podgy Plum. 'And we're taking you as a hostage.'

Timid Thomas turned as white as the full moon. 'Is it true, Little Captain?' he asked, trembling.

The Little Captain shook his head. 'Perhaps the pirate won't be there at all,' he said and he grasped the helm of the *Neversink* to keep her sailing in the wake of the galleon ship.

But the pirate *was* there.

When the highest tree-tops of Tangleroot Island appeared on the horizon, the anchor chain was unhooked. The enchanted ship veered away, to go on sailing in a great curve out of sight of the island, and the *Neversink* with her empty rafts sailed straight on.

'Two degrees thirty South,' called the Little Captain. 'Tomorrow evening.'

'Two degrees thirty South,' the sailors answered from the galleon. 'Tomorrow evening,' and they waved their caps in farewell, except of course for crooked Ben, who had no hands free.

Tangleroot Island looked like a wood washing its feet in the middle of the sea. The tree trunks each had twelve or twenty legs on which they perched, high up. These, of course, were their roots. Straight and crooked and crinkled and stringy and hooped and thick and threadlike. Roots, roots, roots, which you could only crawl through, over the soggy sand. No one could run about on Tangleroot Island.

The pirate was there. He was sitting in a tree, with his wooden leg hanging over a thick branch and a telescope to his one eye. There was a patch over the other.

'Ahoy,' he bellowed when the *Neversink* hove in sight.
'Help!' shrieked Timid Thomas in reply, and slammed the
hatch shut above his head.

The *Neversink* steamed in to shore and the ruffian
almost fell out of the tree with joy.

'Years,' he cried. 'Years I've been sitting on the lookout,
and at last, at last—'

'Yes,' said the Little Captain, tipping his cap politely,
'we saw you sitting there and we thought "A poor shipwrecked sailor like that must be in need of rescue"!'

'That's kind!' cried the robber. 'That's mighty kind
of you. Scurvyboots will be in your debt for ever, what?'

'Scurvyboots?' asked Marinka. Who's that?'

The pirate pointed a finger at his chest. 'That's me, my
maidie,' he said. 'Scurvyboots is my good self.'

'Oh,' said Podgy Plum, enlightened. 'I thought there
were two of you.'

'Ha ha!' bellowed the pirate. 'It's a long time since there was two of us. A couple of cent ... a couple of years or so.'

'Well,' said the Little Captain, 'then perhaps you would like to sail back with us to the inhabited world?'

'That's as sure as eggs is eggs!' cried Scurvyboots. 'You've got plenty of room, too, with all those rafts, what?'

'Yes,' said Marinka. 'And if you've got any luggage or anything...'

She looked innocently at the sky, as if she knew nothing of any golden treasure, but was thinking simply of a few clothes and a toothbrush, a shoe-horn and a book.

'Now you mention it, young lady,' cried Scurvyboots, as if he had only just thought of it himself, 'I have got a few chests about here. They could come along too. What?'

'Yes, of course,' said Podgy Plum. 'On the bed of nails. They'll be stuck fast there all right.'

Scurvyboots peered with one suspicious eye at Fred's spiky raft bobbing on the water. 'What sort of a crazy thing is that?' he asked.

'Oh,' said Marinka, 'the reason for that is that we hadn't any short nails left when we put it together.'

Scurvyboots laughed so loud that his gold teeth flashed in the sunlight.

'Shall we help you with the chests?' asked the Little Captain.

The pirate seemed to hesitate. 'Right,' he said at last.

They jumped ashore—only Timid Thomas remained hidden in the hold—and followed Scurvyboots who went ahead, bent double, through the roots of the strange island. His wooden leg left a peculiar trail of holes in the soggy sand.

Flies buzzed, gnats stung, birds cawed.

Would there really be a treasure hidden there?...

The Treasure

It was a difficult journey. They had to crawl and slither between the tangle of roots and whenever a gust of wind blew, the roots creaked and groaned like ghosts. And the flies buzzed, the gnats stung and the birds cawed.

'What a good thing Timid Thomas isn't with us,' said Marinka and Podgy Plum to each other.

'What's that?' cried Scurvyboots. 'What's the matter?'

'Oh, nothing,' said Marinka. 'It's very comfortable here, isn't it?'

'You think so!' he said. 'I should very much like to know what you children are up to, alone at sea like this?'

'Oh,' said Podgy Plum, 'we didn't feel like going to school. So here we are, you see.'

'Ha ha!' The bellowing laugh of Scurvyboots made the birds fly up in fright.

The Little Captain pinched Marinka's arm. He thought she ought not to be talking so much. At an almost completely overgrown patch of sand Scurvyboots stopped. 'It must be here,' he muttered. 'Three paces right—' He raked among the tough undergrowth with his wooden leg and hit on something hard.

'Here we are! The tr—err ... chests with my bits, I mean. You can easily creep through there and bring them out, can't you?'

'Oh yes, sir,' said the Little Captain touching his cap respectfully.

The three children made their way with difficulty. The chests lay half buried in the sand and there were seven of them. The wood was weathered, the iron fittings rusty and the locks groaned when they were touched.

'Leave it!' shouted Scurvyboots.

'But we'll have to tip them up, won't we?' called Marinka.

'There's no need for you to look inside!' blared the pirate. 'Keep your nose out of other people's affairs, what?'

'Oh,' said Marinka innocently. 'I thought they were just socks and shirts and things.'

'Y-yes,' stammered Scurvyboots. 'Just bring them out now.'

They were as heavy as lead.

'Oof,' said Podgy Plum. 'Some socks! Must have been knitted out of wire wool.'

It was a terrible labour hauling the chests down to the boat. The three children toiled and heaved and tugged. They got snagged, they got stuck and they had hardly any breath left. Scurvyboots cursed the most frightful pirate curses, and Marinka and Podgy Plum asked each other every time they bumped into anything what the tinkling inside the chests could mean. The raft of nails almost sank under the weight of two chests. The rest were distributed among the other rafts, but when the children tried to load the last chest it shot out of their hands, fell against a tree stump and burst open.

Jingle-jangle, gold coins and gold earrings and gold chains and shining pearls and sparkling precious stones rolled across the ground. One even plumped into the water like a startled frog.

'Hell's bells and buckets of blood!' bellowed Scurvyboots. He turned red with fury right up to his eyepatch and stamped so hard on the ground with his wooden leg that it sank in up to the knee. There he stood, all askew.

'Stupid ninnies! Landlubbers! Varmints!'

The Little Captain touched his cap politely. 'I suppose it's your sailor's pay that you've saved up?' he asked. 'We'll have it back in the chest for you, you'll see.'

The pirate paused. The children must be too stupid to get the point, he thought.

But Timid Thomas in the dark hold of the *Neversink* had grown so curious hearing all the rumpus that he overcame his fear and stuck his head outside.

'Oooooh!' he cried. 'Look at that gold! Is that the pirate's treasure?'

With a roar Scurvyboots had him by the throat and was hauling him into the open like a struggling rabbit. 'Help!' cried Timid Thomas. 'You're tearing my shirt.'

'What do you want me to do, skinnymalink? Want me to hang you from a tree, what?'

'No, no!' screeched Thomas. 'I've got no head for heights.'

'Say that again: *pirate*.'

'No, no!' screeched Thomas. 'You're an honest gentleman. And that's not treasure. That's not gold. That is ... that is ...'

'Well?'

'It's chocolate pretend money, of course,' said Marinka. 'And the beads must be painted rabbit droppings, aren't they, mister?' she asked Scurvyboots sweetly.

The pirate seemed about to burst. But not with rage. He bellowed with laughter, so that the sound echoed past the horizon. Timid Thomas was set on his feet and dived back into the hold. He never wanted to see the pirate again in all his life.

Timid Thomas knew nothing about the plan. Timid Thomas did not know that the pirate was stepping aboard the first raft, next to the chest which had been refilled with his gold. He thought the pirate had been left behind on Tangleroot Island when they sailed away...

'Full speed ahead!' shouted the Little Captain, pulling the steam whistle.

Slowly the convoy began to move, the rafts lying low in the water under the heavy gold and the heavy Scurvyboots. The Little Captain stood at the helm, feet wide apart, eyes on the horizon. 'Two degrees thirty South,' he muttered to himself. 'This evening...'

The Attack

Scurvyboots was whistling a merry pirate tune. He was sitting on the first raft with his arms round one chest of golden treasure, as if it were his sweetheart. The rest of the chests stood on the other rafts and the whole procession was towed slowly along by the *Neversink*.

Tangleroot Island disappeared from view and the Little Captain scanned the horizon.

> 'So now I'm free at last,
> bound for a life of pleasure,
> with seven chests made fast,
> full of my golden tr...'

sang the pirate, but he swallowed back the last word, because the children must not guess. At the first port of call he would go ashore as a rich man, ha ha! But the speck which appeared on the horizon towards evening was not a port. It was a sailing ship, ha ha!

Scurvyboots turned pale.

The Little Captain beamed. 'Two degrees thirty South,' he muttered. 'Just right.'

The sailing ship came nearer. They could see her flag now: a black one with a skull on it.

'That's rich,' grumbled Scurvyboots, 'bumping right into that one!' He put his hands to his mouth and shouted to the Little Captain: 'The pirate won't hurt you, see! There's only one man on board, and he can't lift a finger, ha ha!'

It was really rather a good joke, thought Scurvyboots. 'Just sail close alongside!' he shouted.

The Little Captain did so—not because Scurvyboots told him to, but because that was the plan.

'Ahoy!' bellowed Scurvyboots, with a false grin. 'Still sailing all right, crooked Ben? Not got sticky hands from the wheel?'

But scarcely had he shouted to the lonely skipper on the galleon when his grin froze. He turned still paler, as five stalwart sailors suddenly sprang into sight from the cabin of the enchanted ship, threw ropes and nets with hooks on them over the rail, and boarded the *Neversink* and the rafts.

'Help, help!' yelled Podgy Plum and Marinka, to make it look genuine.

But Scurvyboots had no intention of giving himself up so easily. He drew a rusty sword and began to lay about him vigorously with it. The rafts had been pushed together during the boarding and the sailors jumped across them.

'*Kssht!*' went Dirk. 'We'll be having you!' shouted Titch. 'Hit, then!' mocked Gus. 'Get him, lads!' added Fred. And Max advanced with balled fists.

'Ha ha!' bellowed Scurvyboots. 'Come on, then,' and he made his sword sing through the air.

The sailors rushed him, but Scurvyboots jumped to the afterdeck of the *Neversink* and a fierce fight began.

Swish, swash, clang! The rusty sword struck again and again on the metal of the *Neversink* instead of on the sailors, because they moved like quicksilver. But they could not catch Scurvyboots. When Max tried he was almost beheaded, it was only because he ducked so quickly that the six-bucket funnel was—*clonkety-clonk*—one bucket shorter.

'This is taking too long for me,' said Marinka, who was watching with Podgy Plum. 'Hang on a minute.'

Marinka did something quite simple. She opened the hatch to the hold. And when a new attack came and Scurvyboots stepped backwards he fell straight in.

'Hurrah!' shouted the sailors.

But there was one thing Marinka had not thought of—Timid Thomas, who was still hiding in the hold.

When the terrible pirate with his rusty sword and his wooden leg fell in on top of him, Thomas gave the most ghastly yell of his whole life. And he made the highest leap of his whole life. Up through the hatch, so high that he did not land on the deck of the *Neversink* but on the sailing ship alongside.

'Help!' he screamed. 'Help, help, I'm going to be beheaded,' and he ran towards the only man he could see: crooked Ben at the helm. He would protect him. 'Help me!' cried Thomas and flew to crooked Ben's arms as if the sailor were his big, strong father.

What Thomas clasped was not the arms of Ben but the spokes of the wheel. And Ben was so blind with fury at the wicked pirate who had let him sail around for all those years on the enchanted ship, that he forgot everything else and stormed onto the *Neversink* with flying fists to pay Scurvyboots back.

He took such a violent leap that the boarding ropes parted and the five sailors had the greatest difficulty in holding him back.

'Mate!' they roared. 'Mate, how did you get loose all at once?'

Only then did crooked Ben look down at his hands. They were still clenched in fists, but no longer clasped by magic on the wheel—

'B-b-b ...' was all he could get out.

At that moment an anguished screech made them all look up.

The galleon, now that the ropes had parted, was beginning to drift gently away on the evening wind and there was just one figure on board. A small figure, tugging fiercely at the great spoked wheel because he could no longer get his hands off it.

'Help, what can I do?' came the anguished cry again.

Timid Thomas had taken over the enchanted wheel.

Poor Thomas

'Help!' screeched Timid Thomas.
'Help, what can I do? The wheel is
sticking to me. I can't get my hands off.'

The wind made the sails flap. The enchanted ship
drifted farther and farther away with Thomas on board.

'Fall away!' yelled crooked Ben from the *Neversink*.

'Tack!' shouted Dirk.

'Turn the helm!' yelled Titch. 'To starboard!'

'To port!' yelled Fred.

Timid Thomas did them all at once. He turned the
wheel so hard that he had to turn himself with it in order
not to get his arms tied in a knot. The wind took hold of
the sails. They bulged like white bellies, the ropes creaked
and the ship began to sail faster, away from the *Neversink*.

'Full speed ahead!' ordered the Little Captain at the
top of his voice.

Podgy Plum blew the furnace up so hard that he looked
as red as the glowing coals. Marinka shoved at the rail,
as if that might help, the sailors jumped onto their rafts
and helped to paddle with their hands. But the chests of
gold weighed heavily, and there was not even room for
Fred on the bed of nails. They advanced too slowly, the

galleon could not be overtaken. Thomas's voice grew fainter and fainter. All they could hear was ' 'Elp, 'elp' as the H was blown away by the wind.

'The boy is playing the fool,' said Max. 'All he's got to do is turn her into the wind.'

'You just explain that to him, mate,' said the others, panting as they paddled.

Max did not even try. The white sails of the enchanted ship were no bigger now than a handkerchief waving in the distance. Timid Thomas's moans melted in the moaning of the wind. Timid Thomas was poor Thomas now, doomed to sail for ever across the seven seas of the world, clamped by magic to the helm of the pirate's enchanted ship.

The Little Captain took off his cap.

Marinka wiped away a tear. 'I've always nagged at him so much,' she sniffed.

Podgy Plum said: 'Let's go home first and put the sailors and the rafts and the treasure ashore, then we'll sail out again to find him.'

'Good idea,' said Marinka, 'and we'll put the pirate ashore too.'

The pirate! Yes! They had almost forgotten him. He was still sitting in the hold of the *Neversink*, and crooked Ben was sitting on top of the hatch to hold it down. Crooked Ben's eyes were blazing with anger. 'We'll get him,' he repeated.

'We've got him,' said Marinka. 'He might as well swab the deck. On his hands and knees, because the swabber has gone overboard.'

'He's not coming out of the hold,' said crooked Ben menacingly, 'until we're in the home port and the whole police force has been turned out.'

They were not there yet. The *Neversink* had to put out all her strength to tow the heavy rafts. The ship's engine knocked and groaned, the cog wheels ground and grated, the pistons clanked and the bathtub, which was the furnace, quivered with the effort.

'It's not going to burst, is it?' asked crooked Ben, who had had nothing to do with engines for many years.

'Don't blow the furnace up too hard, Podgy,' warned the Little Captain, for safety's sake. 'The bathtub is pretty old by now.'

Their misery over Timid Thomas was interrupted now and then by cries of joy from the rafts. The sailors were rummaging through the gold chests and coming across some lovely objects.

'Take a look at this! What a pretty necklace! Real diamonds these are. For my sister!'

'Here, a George III sovereign. My nephew collects coins. Dig in!'

And each time a furious answering yell came from the hold as Scurvyboots heard the treasure of Tangleroot Island slipping away under his nose.

'Hold your tongue,' crooked Ben shouted downwards. He did not budge from his seat on the hatch.

'It's all mine!' a hollow voice shouted up.

'Yes, yes, honestly plundered, what?'

But the Little Captain shouted to the sailors that they would have to give it all up. 'It's not yours either,' said he.

So they sailed on, the Little Captain at the helm, feet wide apart, eyes on the horizon, in the hope that the galleon might loom up again. But Timid Thomas had no idea how to steer. He was far away when they reached the harbour of Siliku, where they took on water and coal and flour for the pancakes.

And that was lucky, because they were only just inside the harbour walls when a tearing hurricane broke loose.

Poor Thomas ... He could not sail into any port with the enchanted ship. The hurricane struck her on the open sea with the force of a thousand fists jerking at her masts and pounding on her hull. The ropes howled, the sails flapped like thunder, the masts bent like blades of grass and the sea poured foaming across the deck. If Thomas had not been held to the wheel by magic he would certainly have been washed overboard.

Soon the seas were as high as skyscrapers and Thomas felt sick, as if he had been in a lift. 'Oh, *bloulk*!' he burst out.

Then came the highest wave of all. The galleon was snatched up almost into the clouds and dumped down again on something hard. The centre mast fell with a deafening crash and then there was a ghastly silence.

The enchanted ship was stranded and Timid Thomas lay buried under the sail, his hands still on the enchanted helm, and knew no more...

Journey's End

When the storm died down the *Neversink* sailed out of the harbour of Siliku with her train of sailors and golden treasure in tow, homeward bound. Crooked Ben had not moved from his seat on the hatch and the pirate Scurvyboots sat growling furiously in the hold.

Three days later, though it was hard to believe, the dunes came in sight. The home port! And the wind was with them and there was not a cloud in the sky.

After six adventures the Little Captain's boat came sailing home at long, long last, with six rescued seamen.

Marinka and Podgy Plum stood on the foredeck thinking about poor Thomas who would probably never come home again...

'Look,' said Podgy, 'it was off that high dune. The *Neversink* was lying on top of it when the back-to-front wave came and we sailed away with it to sea.'

He pointed and then his mouth fell wide open.

On the top of the dune lay—a ship. A crumpled wreck with broken masts and ragged sails and ropes. All around her on the dunes the place was full. Full of people.

'Little Captain!' shouted Podgy, but the Little Captain had already seen.

'Thomas is stranded,' he said, much moved.

'And all the people are there,' cried Marinka.

It was true. The whole village had run out to see the wreck which had been dumped down on the high dune.

When the *Neversink* sailed into harbour with her steam whistle shrilling there was no one standing on the quayside. No one, that is, but a single lonely figure.

Old Salty.

The tears ran down the old sea-dog's cheeks as he pressed the Little Captain to his chest. 'Have you saved them all, my lad? Do I see right, all of them?'

Gus, Dirk, Max, Titch, Fred and crooked Ben jumped onto the quay. The old salt looked dimly at them through misty eyes.

'Mates,' he exclaimed hoarsely. 'Mates, together again, after the the fearful storm and shipwreck which split us up... Mates... Six tots to celebrate! Doubles! And a triple for myself. And lemonade for the brave rescuers!'

But at that moment the iron hatch of the *Neversink* rattled. The hatch flew open and with a ferocious leap Scurvyboots came into sight. He shot overboard onto the shore, and before crooked Ben could grasp how stupid he had been, the pirate had disappeared, zig-zagging among the houses.

'Here!' yelled the sailors, setting off after him.

'Here!' yelled all the people who had been standing round the wreck of the magic ship. They had been shouting 'Here' for three days already, because there was a cabin boy on board who would not come off. Thomas, of course. The boy who had run away from home months before. Where on earth had he suddenly sprung from now?

But Timid Thomas did not get off. 'I'm kept here by magic,' he howled, over and over again.

No one could free him. Not his parents, however hard they wheedled and promised not to punish him. Not the schoolmaster, however fiercely he waved his wicked stick or promised ten out of ten in his report. Not even the strongest men.

Poor Thomas.

That was why no one had seen the *Neversink* sail in and no one had paid any attention to the steam whistle.

But now, when a pirate with an eyepatch and a wooden leg suddenly came storming ashore, roaring fiercely, everyone began to jostle each other aside.

'My ship!' bellowed Scurvyboots. 'My ship! Who got her into this state? Who let her run aground? What nincompoop was it? I'll have him!'

He jumped onto the deck and bore down on Thomas with a furious snarl.

Thomas yelled, but that was not necessary. The great fists of the pirate landed fair and square on the spokes of the wheel and in that instant he was caught.

Which was just as it should be.

On his own ship, undergoing his own punishment for his own acts of piracy.

Timid Thomas jumped into his mother's arms. 'I shall never run away again,' he sobbed. 'Ne-ever.'

In procession they made their way to the harbour. They held such a feast as had never been held before. Old Salty and the six sailors hoisted the Little Captain on their shoulders and jigged around with him. Podgy Plum and Marinka told all their adventures, on the Island of Evertaller, on the volcano island with the tame wild animals, in the misty city with the Grim Ruler, in Father Bluecrab's sea garden, in the land of the towers and the seven hard labours and finally on Tangleroot Island, with the treasure.

The pirate's golden treasure!

It was examined, passed from hand to hand, but the Little Captain said: 'We must give it back.'

'To whom?'

'To the people it belongs to.'

'How are you going to find them?'

To that the Little Captain made no answer. But in the middle of the night, when the Little Captain was gazing out to sea, a mysterious great wave came. A back-to-front wave. It plucked the enchanted ship off the dune and carried her and Scurvyboots back out to sea. Battered as she was, she sailed away.

'One day you'll be released,' murmured the Little Captain. 'When the gold has been given back.' He looked thoughtfully at the seven heavy chests standing on the quay...

THE LITTLE
CAPTAIN AND THE
PIRATE TREASURE

The Pirate Treasure

The *Neversink* was lying in harbour and the Little Captain was sitting in the cabin. No fire burned under the boiler, no smoke was coming out of the six-bucket funnel, there was no one on deck, there was no one in the hold. The Little Captain was completely alone on his silent boat.

The Little Captain was reading.

He was reading an old, crumpled, yellowed piece of paper which he had found in one of the seven treasure chests he had seized from the pirate Scurvyboots on his last voyage.

The Little Captain wanted to return the seven chests honestly. Not to the pirate, of course, because he had stolen them from someone. But from whom? To whom did the treasure really belong?

The Little Captain scratched his head under his cap, and he read the old, yellowed, crumpled piece of paper through once more: 'To the Great Lord of Fear and Terror', it said, and underneath that:

> 'Herewith the seven chests. Each one is
> filled with treasure: crystal bunnies,

> copper, silver, rubies red,
> diamonds, bigger than your head.
> The sixth oak chest is filled with gold,
> but luck is what the seventh holds.
> I send them to you, sir, by sea,
> and as for theft, rely on me!
> A thieving hand would, through my spell,
> be clamped for ever to the wheel.'

Under these lines there was a jumble of noughts and crosses and lines and dots. They were the writer's signature, but the Little Captain could not read it.

'Who could that be?' thought the Little Captain. 'And who is the Great Lord of Fear and Terror?' That was where the treasure had to go, he realized, but who was he, and how was the Little Captain to find out where the lord lived?

He took off his cap to help him think, but put it on again at once, because he heard footsteps on the deck and a captain must look neat and tidy when he has visitors.

The visitor was old Salty.

'Well, Little Captain,' said Salty. 'What are you going to do with the seven chests?'

'Give them back,' said the Little Captain.

'Yes, but to whom?' asked Salty.

The Little Captain gave him the old, yellowed and crumpled piece of paper and Salty began to read. Salty read it through three times, sucking so hard on his pipe that the cabin was filled with blue smoke.

'Well, well,' he muttered at last, 'that fits.'

'What fits?' asked the Little Captain.

'The signature,' said Salty, 'it's the signature of a wizard. He's the one who sent the chests off long ago, across the sea, and then Scurvyboots stole them. Ha ha! And as a punishment he's stuck to his ship for good now.'

The Little Captain nodded.

'So the chests,' murmured Salty, 'were on their way to the Great Lord of Fear and Terror. That's where you're going to take them, is it?'

The Little Captain nodded. 'They were meant for him,' he said.

Salty nodded too. 'Yes,' he said, 'the Great Lord of Fear and Terror. Hm! Don't go there, Little Captain.'

'What?' cried the Little Captain. 'Do you know who he is? Do you know where he lives? Do you know where I can find him?'

'Sure as ninepence,' said Salty, 'sure as ninepence. But you mustn't go there, my boy, because the Great Lord of Fear and Terror lives in the Misty East. And you won't get your ship into any harbour in the Misty East. They have copper cannons and they sink anything strange with their copper cannons.'

'Oh,' said the Little Captain. 'But they can't sink the *Neversink*.'

'That's what you think, my boy,' said Salty.

'That's what I *know*,' said the Little Captain.

Salty was silent.

'I would like to save Scurvyboots, too,' said the Little Captain. 'When I have returned the treasure he will be released from the bewitched wheel.'

Salty was silent.

'I shall leave tomorrow,' said the Little Captain, 'for the Misty East.'

Then Salty took off his cap. 'I knew it,' he said quietly, 'I knew you would go, after all, Little Captain. Shall I help you load the chests?'

'Thank you,' said the Little Captain.

The chests were still standing on the quay and there were a great many people standing round them, and inquisitive children too.

'Can we help?' asked Marinka.

'Much too heavy for girls,' cried Podgy Plum.

'This one doesn't weigh anything!' cried Marinka. She shook one of the chests to and fro. 'Haha, this one's empty!' she jeered.

That was the seventh chest.

'Keep off!' cried Salty. 'There's good luck in that one.'

Timid Thomas was there too. Timid Thomas didn't help, but he opened his eyes wide when he heard about the seventh chest.

Night had already fallen before the job was done.

'I shall sail tomorrow morning,' said the Little Captain, 'before sunrise...!'

On the Way

When the first cock began to crow in the little port between the dunes, it was joined by another sound: a trumpet.

Ta-ran-ta-ra! It sounded in the clear morning air: the copper trumpet of the Little Captain. The *Neversink* was about to set sail.

The little boat, laden with seven chests full of treasure, lay deep in the water, but when the Little Captain slipped her moorings, echoing footsteps resounded on the quayside.

'Hi, stop!' called two voices. 'Little Captain! Wait a minute, we're coming too!'

She came tripping along like a butterfly—Marinka—and like a butterfly she flew on to the deck.

'Oh,' said the Little Captain. 'But I'm going a long, long way. To the Misty East.'

'I know,' said Marinka. 'We've brought everything with us.'

She pointed to Podgy Plum, who was coming round the corner, puffing like a steam engine. He was carrying a suitcase, a bag, a flour sack, a frying-pan, a telescope, a spare pair of trousers and a fishing rod. And every few seconds one of these things fell to the ground so that every few seconds Podgy Plum had to stoop to pick it up again.

'Get moving, slow-coach!' cried Marinka.

'Yes but ...' the Little Captain began.

'No "yes buts",' said Marinka. 'You've got to have someone to bake the pancakes and someone to blow up the fire, haven't you?'

'Well, yes,' said the Little Captain, 'but ...'

'And we're on holiday,' said Marinka.

Podgy Plum stepped aboard.

Marinka was already tugging at the steam whistle.

The Little Captain took his place behind the wheel.

'Boiler ten degrees atmospheric pressure!' cried Podgy Plum, blowing the flames higher still.

'Batter stirring!' cried Marinka from the galley, cracking an extra egg into it.

'Full steam ahead!' cried the Little Captain, standing steady at the helm, feet apart, eyes fixed on the harbour entrance. So began the voyage of the gallant little boat *Neversink* to the Misty East. In the hold were the seven chests filled with treasure which had to be taken to the Great Lord of Fear and Terror.

'Oh, never mind,' said Marinka. 'Of course he'll be just a nice man and perhaps he'll let us keep something, something gold, you know, because we're bringing it back so honestly.'

The Little Captain was silent. He was thinking about the copper cannons.

'Well,' said Podgy Plum, 'if he isn't nice, we'll just sail away. He won't get anything. We'll keep it all for ourselves. We'll be nice and rich.'

The Little Captain shook his head. 'What about Scurvyboots?' he asked. 'He would never be released if we did that.'

Marinka did not think that was too terrible. 'That nasty pirate,' she said. 'Come and have a look, Podgy,' she said, 'see what's in the treasure chests, see how rich we're going to be?'

'Keep away from them!' cried the Little Captain, but the two children had already slipped through the hatch into the hold and the Little Captain was left standing thoughtfully behind the wheel.

The sea was rocking gently, the wind was whispering sweet words, as if it could never get angry, and the air was as blue as a peacock's neck.

'Hey!' came Podgy Plum's voice as his head appeared through the hatch. 'Hey, Little Captain, there's an animal in one of the chests.'

'Have you looked inside, then?' asked the Little Captain.

'No,' said Podgy Plum. 'We can hear it. We can hear it scrabbling and yammering and sighing.'

The Little Captain switched off the engine and fixed the wheel and followed Podgy Plum into the hold.

Marinka was standing by the chest. It was the seventh chest. Seven sighs came from it.

'Must be a tiger,' said Marinka.

But it was not a tiger.

As the lid slowly opened a crack, a pale little face appeared and a thin little voice asked: 'Am I in Lollipop Land at last?'

It was Timid Thomas.

'Deck-swabber!' cried Marinka. 'How did you get in there?'

'You made a fool of me!' moaned Thomas. 'It's not a lucky chest at all. It's an unlucky chest. Look where I've got to now!'

'On to the *Neversink*,' said the Little Captain.

'And I didn't want to go to sea!' wailed Timid Thomas.

'Don't worry,' said Marinka comfortingly. 'We'll be landing again very soon. And then you can go and visit the Great Lord of Fear and Terror.'

'Wh-wh-who, wh-wh-what? I want to go home!' whined Timid Thomas, quaking.

'Then in you dive and swim back!' cried Podgy Plum.

But it was much too far. The blue sea lay round about them, the home port was out of sight and the *Neversink* steamed on, on her way to the Misty East.

Sobbing, Timid Thomas swabbed the deck.

Singing, Marinka baked pancakes.

Panting, Podgy Plum blew up the fire under the boiler. And while the Little Captain stood steering and peering, he was thinking to himself: 'Odd, that, the seventh chest, the lucky chest, quite empty ... or is Timid Thomas the luck?...'

Brave Marinka

The *Neversink* had already sailed across three blue seas and put in to thirteen ports: Siliku and Proosht and Cali ... but we don't have to name them all. Each port lay closer to the Misty East and in each port the people knew more about the Misty East.

'Don't go there,' said the old salts on the quays.

'You can only land at night, when the moon is down,' said the smugglers in the pubs.

'They'll blow your brains out,' said the old sea lawyers on the park benches.

The Little Captain nodded at whatever they said. 'I know,' he said, 'with copper cannons.'

'C-c-copper c-cannons?' chattered Timid Thomas whenever he heard them. 'I want to go home!'

But Marinka bought flour for the pancakes, Podgy Plum bought coal for the furnace under the boiler and the Little Captain bought charts in order to find the way.

And then they sailed on, to the place where the sun rises like a red ball from the waves every morning, to the east, the Misty East.

And one day they saw it lying there, far ahead on the horizon. Tall blue mountains, with green palm trees and white palaces, and under them a row, and then another row, and yet another row of glittering lights.

They were the sun's rays flashing from the copper cannons. They had just been polished. 'They're going to fire!' cried Timid Thomas, fleeing for the hold.

'You go and sit in the lucky chest,' cried Marinka. 'They won't get you there.'

But the *Neversink* was still too far off to be fired on and the Little Captain lowered the anchor.

'The lucky chest,' he muttered thoughtfully. 'That's an idea!'

'What do you mean, Little Captain?' asked Marinka.

Then the Little Captain told them his plan. He said: 'If the Great Lord of Fear and Terror knew we were bringing treasure he would not let the copper cannons fire on the *Neversink*.'

'No,' said Podgy Plum. 'That's obvious. But he doesn't know.'

'And so,' said the Little Captain, 'one of us must go ashore to tell him.'

'Ashore?' asked Podgy Plum. 'How? Swim?'

'No,' said the Little Captain. 'In the lucky chest.'

'Aha!' cried Podgy Plum. 'Timid Thomas!'

'No,' said the Little Captain. 'Timid Thomas is too timid.'

'Well,' said Podgy Plum. 'I'm too fat. I would sink, chest and all. You go, Little Captain.'

But Marinka, who had heard everything, cried: 'Oh no, a captain always stays with his ship!' And then Marinka said: 'I'll go.'

She was a brave Marinka.

The Little Captain doffed his cap to her and said: 'Marinka, the lucky chest will drift into harbour on the tide. That will give you an hour. Then it will be ebb tide and it must bring the chest back again. We'll be waiting for you here.'

'Right,' said Marinka. 'An hour is enough. The Great Lord of Fear and Terror will be glad to hear about the treasure. I don't need to be afraid of him.'

She turned and went into the cabin. There she put on her prettiest butterfly dress, tied three red ribbons in her long hair and reappeared dressed like a princess.

Timid Thomas had to help lower the chest into the water.

'Goodbye Shivershanks,' said Marinka, and flitting like a butterfly over the railing, she was in the chest in one bound.

'Just like a little wooden house on the water!' called Marinka. 'Shut the lid and shove off!' A moment later the chest was bobbing slowly into port on the waves of the incoming tide. The lid was slightly ajar, as an air-hole, and as a peep-hole for brave Marinka.

Three little figures stood staring after her over the bows of the *Neversink*.

'Lucky chest,' murmured the Little Captain. 'What does it really mean?'

'Un-un-unlucky chest ...' quavered Timid Thomas beside him. 'It b-brought m-me bad luck. Didn't it?'

'Oh, stop nagging!' cried Podgy Plum. 'You're a bit of bad luck yourself, wherever you manage to crawl! Marinka will get on fine. You'll see.'

They waited one hour.

They waited two hours.

They waited three hours.

The sun crept further and further across the blue sky. The mountains and the palm trees and the white palaces of the Misty East became mistier and mistier in the late afternoon light. There was not a movement to be seen, not a sound to be heard, even the gulls were not crying.

But just as Timid Thomas was beginning to snivel, the Little Captain said: 'There it comes.'

And sure enough, there was the chest, bobbing out of the harbour on the ebb tide, no bigger than a pin prick. Slowly, very slowly ...

'It's lying very high,' said Podgy Plum.

'Marinka is light,' said the Little Captain.

'The luck's gone out of it,' wailed Thomas.

He was right. When at last, at last, they were able to land the chest and open the lid, there seemed to be nothing inside it. No Marinka, no luck.

But there was something inside it: on the bottom lay a sheet of paper and on the paper someone had written in trembling letters (the Little Captain read it out): 'Sail into the harbour at midnight. The Great Lord of Fear and Terror has been ...'

The last word had been turned into an unreadable splodge by the sea water.

Fear and Terror?

Three old men sat fishing on the outermost point of the quay. They were doing their best, but the fish did not want to bite.

'Look,' said one. 'I'm making my float turn and turn, but those mackerel down there aren't hungry.'

'Look,' said the second, 'I'm making my float dance and dance, but there is a lemon sole down there, fast asleep.'

'Look,' said the third, 'a chest.'

The three old men forgot their floats and they all watched the chest come floating in on the tide and being bumped against the quay by the waves.

'Perhaps there's a monkey inside,' said one.

'Or dried prunes,' said the second.

But the third man lifted the lid and Marinka stepped out of the chest.

'Didn't think of that, did you?' she said. 'Didn't expect to find me in there!'

'No,' said the fishermen, 'we hadn't thought of that. What a brave little girl. Or are you a mermaid?'

'I'm not, actually,' said Marinka. 'And I must go to the palace. Can you show me the way?'

'Of course,' said the first little man.

'It's over there,' said the second little man.

But the third little man said: 'They won't let you in.'

'Oho,' said Marinka. 'I've got a message for the Great Lord of Fear and Terror.'

'The Great Lord of Fear and Terror?'

'Aha, ehee, oho!' they began to laugh like mad. 'You really are a mermaid, aren't you? You don't know anything about the affairs of men.'

'I am Marinka,' said Marinka.

'Yes, yes! Off to the palace, quickly,' said the three old men, turning back to their three floats. All three had a bite.

Marinka walked to the palace.

It was big and white, being made of marble, and it stood on eighty-seven pillars. The streets leading to it were crowded, but all the people looked miserable or cross. Their clothes were tattered and there was only one bun on the shelf at the baker's shop.

'It's not very jolly here,' thought Marinka, tugging at the copper bell of the palace.

But the door did not open. Through a shutter, a voice called, 'Not at home! And there's no more money!'

The shutter closed.

'Never say die,' thought Marinka, tugging at the copper bell again, twice, very loudly.

'NOT AT HOME!' the voice shouted through the closed shutter, but Marinka stood on her toes and shouted back: 'I've got some money for you!'

There was immediate silence. Then the shutter opened. 'Wha-whadidyousay?'

'Listen,' said Marinka, 'I've come to bring you seven chests full of treasure for the—'

The palace door flew open and Marinka was drawn inside by a man, large as life, in an apron, large as life, covered with spots and tears.

'Is this a poor country?' asked Marinka.

'Poor, poor, poor,' replied the palace lackey. 'But the cannons are polished.'

'I saw that,' said Marinka. 'But if you start shooting with them you'll get no chests full of treasure.'

The lackey's eyes began to sparkle. 'Where are they?' he asked.

'Shan't tell you that yet,' said Marinka. 'First take me to the Great Lord of Fear and Terror. He lives here, doesn't he?'

A wave ran down the apron. The man seemed to go limp and leaned against the marble wall for support.

'Fear and Terror,' he whispered. 'No no ... yes ... yes ... come with me, my girl.'

Before Marinka knew what was happening he was pulling her by one arm, further into the palace. Up marble steps with golden banisters, through empty

rooms with mirror floors, along passages of shimmering crystal. At last they came to a door with three thick bolts and three thick curtains and Marinka vanished behind that. Behind the thick curtains, brave Marinka vanished without trace. No more to be seen, no more to be heard—except a chattering of teeth. That was all.

An hour later the three fishermen on the quayside heard running footsteps coming closer. It was the lackey in his apron. But instead of Marinka, he had brought a letter with him.

'The chest!' he cried.

The three fishermen pointed to the chest.

The lackey put the letter inside and pushed the chest off on the ebb tide which carried it out to sea where the *Neversink* lay at anchor.

And when the Little Captain had landed the chest and read the letter through three times and read it out to Podgy Plum and Timid Thomas three times, he said: 'I don't understand. Why didn't Marinka come herself? And what's the matter with the Great Lord of Fear and Terror?'

'We'll soon see,' said Podgy Plum. 'We have to sail in at midnight.'

The setting sun made the copper cannons in the harbour shine with a reddish glow and Timid Thomas began to moan softly ...

The Copper Cannon

'Anchor aweigh!' cried the Little Captain.

It was pitch-black night. The half moon had just gone down and all you could see of the stars was the Great Bear and in the harbour there were only three lights.

'I have to steer straight for them,' said the Little Captain. 'Then I'll be safe in harbour.'

Podgy Plum blew up the fire under the boiler and the ruddy light of the flames shone on Timid Thomas.

Timid Thomas was standing on the foredeck in order to be able to shout *whoa!* if he saw a rock sticking out of the waves. But his teeth were chattering so hard that he would only have been able to shout *k-k-kock*, instead of rock.

'Are you as cold as all that, Thomas?' asked Podgy Plum between two puffs.

'K-k-k ...' Timid Thomas replied.

'Oh,' said Podgy Plum, 'do you mean the c-c-copper c-c-cannons? Well, if they start firing, you'll soon get warm.'

Timid Thomas would have liked to give a shrill scream, but he did not dare do even that. And the *Neversink* sailed calmly into harbour at half power, while the Little Captain stood at the helm, feet apart, his eyes on the three little lights.

They were the lights on the quay, and they were slowly coming nearer. Was there anyone watching, or did it only look like it? There was not a movement to be seen, not a sound to be heard. Except for the soft dunk-dunk-dunk of the ship's engine and now and then the wailing whistle of the six-bucket funnel.

And then it happened.

A tremendous explosion, all round the harbour. Boom, thunder and crash of fire, hissing and whistling in the air, and a blinding light.

Timid Thomas's shrill scream burst out now at full strength, but it was quickly smothered because Thomas and his scream jumped into the hold and slammed the hatch shut behind them.

Poor little Thomas! He could not see the splendid fireworks going off over the harbour. Red and green and blue and yellow rockets rushed upwards and burst in a thousand flowers of light. Screamers, crackers, Roman candles, golden rain, Catherine wheels, Chinese parasols and Japanese flashes put the whole town, harbour, houses and all in a dazzling glow of light.

It was the copper cannons.

But instead of aiming cannonballs at the *Neversink*, they were shooting fireworks into the air as if shouting 'Hurrah!' to the *Neversink*. And there, suddenly, came a real hurrah from the waterside.

'Oooh!' cried Podgy Plum. 'Look at all the people! The quay is covered with them. The jetty is wobbling!'

It was a glorious welcome for the *Neversink* at the midnight hour, with many a pom-pom-pom and choruses of ladies, with flags and trumpets and with a torch dance by the loaders and unloaders.

'They must be pleased with the treasure,' said Podgy Plum.

'Yes,' said the Little Captain.

He brought his boat in alongside the jetty and Podgy Plum tied up by the light of the torches.

'Thomas!' he shouted, banging on the hatch. 'Come out now, Timid Thomas!'

Timid Thomas's face was paler than the moon. 'A-aren't we dead yet, then?' he asked.

'Of course not,' said Podgy Plum, and they stepped ashore, where a group of Misty Eastern reed-pipes, fiddles and mouth-organs were playing a song of welcome.

Timid Thomas was speechless. 'Wh-where is Marinka now?' he asked tearfully.

Marinka was nowhere to be seen, but a big man in an apron came over to them and bowed to the ground.

'Are you the Great Lord of Fear and Terror?' asked the Little Captain.

The man staggered back. 'N-n-ssst!' he uttered. 'I will conduct you.'

He snapped his fingers and twelve soldiers marched up. They were carrying twelve spears and twelve torches. Six of them went to stand in front of the *Neversink*, grim-faced, to guard the treasures in the hold, for there were many folk about. The other six took the Little Captain, Podgy Plum and Timid Thomas along with them to the white palace on its eighty-seven pillars.

There was a great crowd to be pushed through. The Misty Easterners looked on, in their ragged clothes, their faces questioning in the red light of the torches.

The door to the palace stood open. They walked along marble corridors, through halls with mirror floors, along crystal passages, through the door with the three bolts, and there the three thick curtains were slowly drawn apart.

A vast room lay before them, dimly lighted by a pair of flickering tallow lamps. Here and there stood an old chair.

'I think it's horrid here,' quavered Timid Thomas.

He was ready to run away, but someone came towards them out of the half-darkness.

'Hello, hello,' cried a voice. 'Are you here at last?'

It was Marinka.

'Marinka!' Thomas fell sobbing on her neck, but Marinka pushed him away. 'That's not etiquette at court,' she said sharply. 'Come on, Little Captain, I will present you.' Marinka pointed to a dais and there, on a battered, worm-eaten wooden throne sat a poor little man with chattering teeth.

The Little Captain removed his cap. 'The Great Lord?' he asked doubtfully, '... of Fear and Terror?'

Before the little man on the throne could answer Marinka burst out: 'What? Better and better!' she cried. 'Haven't you even read my letter? I wrote it down: the Great Lord of Fear and Terror has been dead for ages.'

The First Chest

If only they had known! Then they would not have been so frightened of the Misty East.

Marinka had to laugh. She had not been a prisoner at all: she had been a guardian angel. And now she knew everything.

'Look,' she said, pointing to the battered, worm-eaten, wooden throne on which the poor little man sat with chattering teeth. 'This is the son of the Great Lord of Fear and Terror.'

'Oh,' said the Little Captain.

'He has succeeded his father as Lord of the Misty East,' said Marinka. 'But he's different from his father. His name is different, too. He is called the Poor Lord of Quake and Quiver.'

'You can see that,' said Podgy Plum.

'He's even more timid,' said Marinka, 'than Timid Thomas.'

'Aha,' said Thomas, sticking his timid chest out quite bravely.

The Poor Lord of Quake and Quiver raised his head and looked at the four children from the sea. 'The treasure!' he burst out. 'Where are the chests full of treasure?'

They had not slept all night and Timid Thomas was rubbing his eyes. 'Does he get the lucky chest as well?' he asked the Little Captain. 'With nothing inside?'

'Of course,' said the Little Captain. 'All seven.'

But very soon they were to find out that things were quite different ...

For on the jetty stood the faithful palace lackey in his ragged apron and when the soldiers were about to unload he said:

'One chest.'

'What did you say?' asked the Little Captain.

'Only one chest for the Poor Lord of Quake and Quiver.'

The Little Captain scratched his head under his cap. 'Why?' he asked.

The lackey drew the children after him into the cabin. 'Listen,' he whispered. 'I know all about the treasure. The magician who sent it off long ago put a letter with it, didn't he?'

'Yes,' said the Little Captain.

'The treasure was meant for the Great Lord of Fear and Terror,' said the lackey, 'or ... after his death for his children ...'

'Well?' asked Podgy Plum.

The lackey straightened. 'The treasure is packed in seven chests,' he said. 'Because the Great Lord of Fear and Terror had seven children.'

'Seven?' cried Marinka.

'Seven,' repeated the lackey. 'Six sons and one daughter he had. One chest for each. That's how they have to be split up.'

'Ah,' said the Little Captain. 'I understand.'

'The letter,' whispered the lackey. 'Show me the letter.'

The Little Captain pulled out the old, yellowed and crumpled piece of paper and gave it to the lackey, who began to mumble aloud:

> '... filled with treasure: crystal bunnies,
> copper, silver, rubies red,
> diamonds, bigger than your head.
> The sixth oak chest is filled with gold,
> but luck is what the seventh holds ...'

'Ha,' said the lackey, 'the eldest son has the first choice. The Poor Lord of Quake and Quiver chooses the chest full of diamonds!'

The Little Captain shrugged his shoulders. 'All right by me,' he said. 'And the other chests? Where are the other sons? And the daughter?'

There was a silence. Then, with a wide sweep of the long sleeves of his overall, the lackey pointed round about him.

'Flown away,' he said miserably. 'Flown from the parental nest! They've scattered to the four winds. Three sons to the Deep South, two sons to the Wild West and the daughter, the youngest, to the Far North.'

Again there was silence. Then Marinka said: 'Well well, it's going to be a long way round.'

'Fine!' cried Podgy Plum. 'Then we still don't have to go to school.'

'Boo-hoo!' wept Timid Thomas. 'I wouldn't dare to go so far from home!'

The Little Captain said nothing, the Little Captain stood thinking.

He was thinking of Scurvyboots, the pirate, who had to go on sailing the world on his ship with his hands stuck fast to the helm until the seven chests of treasure had been given back. To the seven children of the Great Lord of Fear and Terror ...

When the *Neversink* sailed silently out of harbour an hour later a single chest was standing on the quay. A chest for the Poor Lord of Quake and Quiver in the Misty East. The other six chests were still on board.

The Ship of the Desert

The south is a very long way off.

You have to sail and sail, across a thousand waves and then a thousand more, and the sun rises higher and higher, the shadows grow shorter, until in the end the sun is standing right above your head. Then all the shadows have gone and it is as hot as a baking-oven.

The Deep South lies even further away than that. You have to tip your head right back in order to see the sun, for the sun stands in the north.

The *Neversink* was on her way towards the Deep South, for somewhere there three of the sons of the Great Lord of Fear and Terror must live. The *Neversink* had six cases of treasure on board and three of them were intended for those sons.

'We must get them there,' said the Little Captain, 'because the pirate Scurvyboots has to be set free.'

'Oh, really!' said Marinka. 'What does the fellow matter to us?'

'I see,' said the Little Captain, 'so you would just let him bob around on his sailing ship for ever? With his hands stuck fast to the helm?'

Marinka gazed at her feet.

'You know quite well,' the Little Captain continued, 'that this is the only way to set Scurvyboots free. By delivering the chests of treasure. To the family of Fear and Terror.'

Marinka bowed her head.

'If I have to sail round the world three times,' said the Little Captain, 'it is my duty as a sailor.'

'Hey,' said Marinka, 'I've lost my shadow.'

'Yes,' cried Podgy Plum, 'I've lost mine too. I expect Timid Thomas has scrubbed them off.'

Timid Thomas hung over the railing with a bucket on a rope, trying to scoop up water. He had to keep the *Neversink's* deck wet against the heat of the sun.

'Shadow gone?' said the Little Captain. 'Then we're right on the equator.'

'The equator?' asked Timid Thomas. 'Is that something bad?' He almost dropped his bucket.

'It's a blue line,' said Marinka. 'And it divides the world into two halves.'

But however hard Thomas stared into the water he could see no line and the *Neversink* sailed on and on. The sun was left behind in the north, the shadows came back and after seventeen days Podgy Plum saw a brown streak in the distance.

'Land!' he cried.

'This must be the Deep South,' thought the Little Captain. He steered straight for it and the brown streak became wavy.

'Lots of little hills!' cried Marinka.

'They're moving!' cried Podgy Plum.

The Little Captain turned off the engine and steered towards the strange land.

'They're not little hills,' he said. 'They're camels. I think the desert begins there.'

And sure enough, when at last the *Neversink* lay bobbing on the last waves of the sea, the children saw an endless expanse of sand before them. Yellow, dazzling sand, as far as the eye could see.

'Timid Thomas?' cried Marinka. 'Have you got your wooden spoon? And the cutters? You could bake some nice biscuits.'

But Timid Thomas didn't dare, because of the camels.

There were ten or so of the humped creatures walking about, rather dreamily, but when they saw the *Neversink* they came inquisitively down to look.

'Do they bite?' asked Podgy Plum.

The Little Captain shook his head. He jumped ashore and thrust the boat's anchor firmly into the sand.

'Come along!' he cried.

Marinka stroked the camels' noses, Podgy Plum patted them on their crooked necks, Timid Thomas was still shivering on deck and the Little Captain was thinking.

'The ship of the desert,' thought the Little Captain. 'We shall have to go still deeper south in order to find the three sons. We might as well change over here from one ship to another.'

That was a good idea. For camels are tremendously strong creatures which can walk through the hot desert for days and days and carry heavy loads as well.

'Listen,' said the Little Captain, 'we'll have to go on overland.'

They nodded.

'And we'll have to take the treasure chests with us,' said the Little Captain. 'We'll go by camel.'

'No,' shrieked Timid Thomas from the *Neversink*. 'Help! I want to go home!'

But whether Timid Thomas shrieked or not, he had to help. All six chests were dragged out of the hold one by one and carried ashore. Each camel was given two to carry, one on each side of his body, with a rope tied over his back.

'We only have to deliver three chests,' said Podgy Plum.

'But we can hardly leave the rest in the hold. What if pirates were to come while we were gone?'

'P-pirates?' quavered Thomas. And he decided that it would be better to stay with the others after all and travel with them by camel.

So the procession set off. Four camels, each with a child on its front hump, and three camels with two chests on each side. The last camel walked crooked, because it had the lucky chest tied on one side and that was always empty ...

Would they find anyone in the endless, endless desert sand?

Mirage

'It keeps rolling!' cried Timid
Thomas. He had been saying
the same thing for hours, for
they had already been travelling
for hours, on their camels, across
the endless desert. The dry, hot, flat,
empty, silent desert sand.

'I'm going to be seasick!' cried Timid Thomas.

'Camel-sick, you mean,' said Marinka. 'Eat a cream
cake. It helps.'

'Oolf' went Timid Thomas, looking as yellow as the
sand.

On they went, deeper and deeper south. Podgy Plum
was puffing with the heat. 'Little Captain,' he asked,
'where do we come out?'

But the Little Captain did not answer. He steered his
camel straight ahead, the reins taut in his hand, his eyes
on the horizon.

On they went, hour after hour after hour.

'I'm stifling with heat,' cried Podgy Plum.

'I'm dying of thirst,' sighed Marinka.

'I want to be sick,' moaned Timid Thomas.

Then the Little Captain called a halt, they dismounted and rested on the burning sand to have something to eat and drink.

'Isn't the sand beautiful,' said Marinka. 'You can write your name all over it—ouch!' She was trying it out with her finger, but it was too hot. A stick worked better. *Marinka was here,*' she wrote in the sand. 'You never know,' she said, 'if they might have to come and rescue us.'

'Rescue?' asked Timid Thomas in a timid voice. 'Th-then are we los ...'

Timid Thomas got no further. His voice stuck in his throat. He stared into the distance with bulging eyes.

'What's the matter, Thomas?' asked Podgy Plum.

But Timid Thomas did not answer. He stood up like a pale ghost, put his hands out in front of him and began to walk. Towards nothing. Towards the far horizon which was nothing but a misty line.

'Thomas?' called Marinka.

'Here!' called Podgy Plum.

But the Little Captain said: 'He's seeing a mirage.'

It was true. Timid Thomas could see something the others could not see. He could see a garden, the most beautiful garden from his most beautiful dream, with waving trees and pretty flowers and pleasant arbours. And with a fountain which spurted cool, fresh, clear water.

It was not really there, the whole garden was not there, but people who journey across the desert and are thirsty from having the hot sun on their heads suddenly see things like that in front of them—in their imagination.

'A mirage,' cried the Little Captain (because that is its name). 'Catch him!'

'But I can't see anything,' said Podgy Plum.

'I mean catch Thomas,' shouted the Little Captain. 'Quick!'

The three of them dragged Timid Thomas back, but the poor little chap began to howl.

'I'm so thirsty! I want to go to the garden. Let me go!'

He tugged, he hit out, he scratched, he bit. Timid Thomas had turned into Thomas the Terror. They could not get him under control, he kept on running away, and in the end the Little Captain said: 'Well, put him in the empty chest.'

It was the only hope.

The three camels with the treasure chests were still lying patiently in the sand. The empty chest, the lucky chest, was opened and Timid Thomas was put inside.

Poor Thomas. It was even hotter there than outside, but however much he shrieked and howled, the lid stayed shut—with a crack for air, of course.

And on they went. Lucky for Thomas, who would otherwise have vanished for ever into the desert; lucky for the camel, which could walk straight now because the chest on one side was just as heavy as the chest on the other side.

The sun began to sink and then it was the Little Captain who gave a shout.

'An oasis!' cried the Little Captain.

'What?' asked Podgy Plum. 'Another dream garden?'

'No,' said the Little Captain. 'This is a real one.'

'Do you know for sure?' asked Marinka. 'Aren't you very thirsty?'

'Oh yes,' said the Little Captain, 'I'm very thirsty, but the palm trees there are real.'

The Little Captain was right. A quarter of an hour later they were standing in the shadow of the leaves and drinking water from the well. Cool, clear water.

'Then is this the garden Timid Thomas saw?' asked Marinka. She opened the lid of the chest. 'Thomas, we're there!'

But Timid Thomas had fallen asleep. He was snoring like an ox.

'Leave him alone,' said the Little Captain. 'He'll wake up on his own soon and then he'll be quite all right again.'

Then night fell, the pitch-black night of the desert, where there is no other light than that of a thousand sparkling stars above your head. Where there is no shadow, for everything is black.

And yet ... shadows were moving about. Creeping shadows, slowly approaching the oasis.

Timid Thomas's Trail

The desert on the way
to the Deep South is not
entirely uninhabited. Here and there are hills with caverns and passages in them and in the caves live robbers. Robbers lying in wait for long-distance travellers, on camels, carrying spoils.

That night two rode out on fast, silent horses, for in the distance they had seen a caravan, a caravan of seven camels.

'It looks as if there are children on the humps,' said one.

'Children? That's nothing!' said the other. 'I can see baggage. I can see chests. Heavy chests. Spoils!'

In the dark night they rode towards the oasis, stealthily—the robbers Borrow and Morrow.

'What shall we do?' asked Morrow. 'Get the whole place in an uproar with enough noise for ten?'

'We'll be like ghosts,' said Borrow. 'We won't make any noise, we'll only take the camels.'

The night breeze rustled softly in the trees as the two shadows crept forward and untied the camels' ropes with swift fingers. The good, patient, obedient creatures got to their feet and followed the two dark figures over the rippling sand.

Without a sound the procession left the oasis.

The three children who were sleeping peacefully beside the well, dreaming of glorious flower gardens with fountains in them, did not even move.

'Spoils!' hissed Morrow. 'We've got the spoils.' He wanted to look inside the chest straight away but Borrow gave him a shove. 'Get your greedy fingers off! Time enough to count it all when we're home again.'

They mounted their horses and drove the camels away into the dim desert.

What the robbers Borrow and Morrow had not noticed was that the lid of one of the chests was slightly open. And that the two timid eyes of a timid little boy were staring out. A boy too timid to shout for help. How could the robbers have known that Timid Thomas had been sleeping inside one of the treasure chests?

When the camel moved off, Timid Thomas woke up with a shock. Timid Thomas yawned, stared through the crack, wanted to yell, but saw the shapes of two ghosts in the darkness which made both yawn and yell stick in his gullet. He wanted to jump out of the chest but dared not, clutched at a branch but it was a dead one, hanging loose on the tree.

The whole chest quivered with Thomas's terror. 'Help!' he wanted to shout. 'Help, help, I'm being stolen and kidnapped.' But not a sound came from his throat. Then he stuck the branch out to wave, but who could see it in the dark night? Not even the robbers.

'Help, help!' But Timid Thomas was not shouting, he was writing. He was writing as Marinka had done, in the sand, with his branch.

The camels plodded on under the thousand, thousand pinprick lights of the stars above the endless desert. Camels with nothing, and camels with chests, and the last camel leaving a strange track behind it. It looked like a doodle on a scribbling-pad.

When the distant sun rose from the yellow sand like a red ball of fire, Podgy Plum woke up. He rubbed his eyes, sniffed, scratched his head and looked about him. 'Hallo,' thought Podgy Plum, 'it looks just as if something that should be there isn't there. But what?' He looked across at the Little Captain, sleeping with his cap over his eyes. He looked at Marinka, rolled up on the sand like a cat. He looked at —

Ah! Suddenly Podgy Plum knew: Timid Thomas wasn't there.

'Thomas!' he shouted. 'Timid Thomas! Where are you?'

'Timid Thomas might be leaning against a tree somewhere,' thought Podgy Plum, but more and more time passed and he failed to appear.

'Hallo!' cried Marinka suddenly, yawning. 'Where are the camels?'

'The *camels*!' Podgy Plum shouted so loudly that the Little Captain was also awakened. 'The camels have gone! And Timid Thomas too!'

The Little Captain got to his feet and looked at the tracks in the sand. 'They're a few hours old,' he said.

'The traitor!' cried Podgy Plum. 'He's made off in the middle of the night with all the treasure.'

'Timid Thomas wouldn't dare do anything like that,' said Marinka.

The Little Captain was following the tracks.

'The creatures wouldn't go off by themselves, would they?' said Podgy Plum. 'We had tied them up securely, too. Someone untied the knots. Who could it have been but Thomas?'

'Well,' said Marinka, 'perhaps he's gone back to the *Neversink* then.'

'No!' cried Podgy Plum. 'I know! He's gone to his garden, of course! To his dream garden.'

The Little Captain was still following the camel tracks. 'That's odd,' he muttered suddenly. 'Look here.'

There were funny scratches in the sand, a sort of quavering line.

'Like doodling,' said Podgy Plum.

But Marinka gave a little shriek. 'There's something there,' she cried. 'Writing! Have a look: you can read it!'

Now the Little Captain and Podgy Plum could see it

too. A quavering line of letters, all joined together, reaching to the horizon: helphelphelphelp ...

'Timid Thomas,' said the Little Captain. 'Timid Thomas and the camels have been kidnapped. By robbers ...'

What the Robbers Forgot

The robbers Borrow and Morrow had a brother. His name was Allmysorrow and he played on his accordion all day long. Allmysorrow was not at all a good robber; he did not even have a horse. He had a donkey, on which he rode backwards, so that he could hold on to its tail.

Allmysorrow never wanted to go out robbing with his brothers. 'You and your donkey!' said Borrow and Morrow. But that didn't worry Allmysorrow. He was not all that keen on getting rich. He preferred to stay at home in the cave where they lived and cook their dinners and play on his accordion and sing the most delightful songs:

> 'The robber's little laddie
> had a shotgun for his play.
> He shot his Mum, he shot his Daddie
> and he grew deafer every day.'

When Borrow and Morrow returned home from their night's outing with the camels Allmysorrow had to help unload the chests and carry them into the cave.

'Heavy, aren't they!' he cried. 'They must be full of sand.'

'Sand, fiddlesticks,' said Borrow.

'Let's have a look,' said Morrow.

They had opened the first chest and were staring, wide-eyed, at the contents.

'Oh, just gold,' said Allmysorrow. 'Where's the music in that?'

They opened the second chest.

'Silver!' cried Borrow and Morrow, their eyes greedy.

'I'd have you know,' said Allmysorrow, 'that I've no intention of polishing all that lot.'

The third chest was full of copper. Allmysorrow did not even bother to look.

The fourth chest glittered with red rubies, but Allmysorrow picked up his accordion. 'What a lot of rubbish,' he said, and began to play a little air.

But when Borrow and Morrow opened the fifth chest and they themselves cried 'Oh, what rubbish!' Allmysorrow got up curiously to have a look.

'Oh,' he cried, 'that's beautiful!'

The chest was full of crystal rabbits.

'You can have that one, then,' said Borrow and Morrow. 'You can have a nice game with it.'

Crystal sings if you tap it gently. Allmysorrow placed the rabbits in a ring and made music on them with his fingers. Pling-plang-plong, they went. Allmysorrow was enchanted.

Then Borrow and Morrow opened the last chest.

That was full of little boy.

'What's this?' cried Morrow.

'What indeed!' cried Borrow. 'A little slave. We can sell him off well.'

Poor Thomas. He was still unable to utter a word. He could not even shout for help; it would not have helped him anyway.

Borrow picked him up out of the chest and Morrow felt his arms.

'Useless little scrag-end,' he said. 'No fat, no muscle. Good for nothing.'

'N-no!' Timid Thomas managed to stammer out at last. 'I shall never do it again.'

'Never do what again?' asked Borrow.

'R-run away,' hiccupped Timid Thomas.

'Run away? Did you run away?'

'I-I-I saw a garden,' said Timid Thomas. 'A very beautiful garden, and then —'

'What?' It was Allmysorrow who shouted. He left his singing rabbits and came over to Thomas. 'A garden with trees and flowers and arbours and a fountain?' he asked.

Timid Thomas nodded palely.

'There you are, you see!' Allmysorrow cried to his brothers. 'You never believed me, did you? When I said I saw the garden! Now what do you say?'

Borrow and Morrow looked at each other. Robbers don't believe in fairy tales, but now that two people had spoken of the mysterious garden in the desert they began to have doubts.

'Who knows,' muttered Borrow.

'We've got enough money now,' whispered Morrow.

'And you wouldn't have to go on being robbers any more,' said Allmysorrow. 'We could go and live there in peace.'

Borrow and Morrow looked at Timid Thomas. 'He can rake leaves,' they said.

'No!' yelled Timid Thomas. 'I want to go back. Back to the Little Captain.'

But the Little Captain was far away. He was standing in the middle of the desert with Marinka and Podgy Plum, shaking his head gloomily.

'We'll never catch up,' said the Little Captain. 'We can follow this helphelphelp trail, but without our camels we'll never overtake the robbers.'

He had realized that this was robbers' work.

All they could do was to return to the oasis. The sun was already beginning to burn.

'Thomas!' sobbed Marinka. 'Treasure!'

'Well,' said Podgy Plum. 'I didn't think Timid Thomas was all that much of a treasure, you know.'

'No!' howled Marinka. 'I mean we've lost Timid Thomas and the treasure.'

'Oh,' said Podgy Plum. 'Well, what now? We can't even get back to the *Neversink*.'

Marinka had not thought of that.

The Little Captain had.

The Little Captain was looking pretty gloomy. They would have to stay at the oasis until another caravan passed by. That might take weeks or months and what would become of Timid Thomas? Now that the treasure chests had been stolen, they would not be able to release Scurvyboots the pirate from his ghost ship, either. The Little Captain had never been so full of gloomy thoughts.

But at that very moment he heard Marinka shouting. Marinka had run ahead and disappeared among the trees of the oasis. 'Left!' she was shouting. 'Left, left!'

The Little Captain and Podgy Plum ran towards her. Marinka was standing at the far end of the oasis, and beside her stood —

'Oh!' said Podgy Plum, 'she was saying "there's one left!"'

For beside Marinka stood the two-humped animal on which Timid Thomas had been riding before he had been packed into the chest.

The robbers had forgotten one camel ...

A Mirror in the Sky

Quicker than light-
ning, the three children
jumped on the camel's
back. The Little Captain sat on the front hump, Marinka
between the two humps and Podgy Plum on the back hump.

'Full steam ahead!' cried the Little Captain, but that
didn't help. The camel was not the *Neversink*.

Podgy Plum blew out his cheeks, but of course the
camel had no furnace to be stoked, either.

'Gee up!' cried Marinka. That was animal talk. The
camel understood that. It rose to its feet and began to
walk, but it walked very slowly and sleepily.

'*Hup hup hup*!' cried Marinka. 'Faster.' She drummed
the animal's sides with her heels. That helped. The
camel began to trot, to canter, to gallop. Marinka's heels
tickled.

The Little Captain steered with his legs clamped fast
on the front hump and his eyes on Timid Thomas's
trail—the helphelphelp trail which led in a quavering
line across the sand to the horizon.

'Faster, faster! *Hup hup hup*!' Marinka went on

encouraging the camel and the good beast galloped on, hour after hour.

'I can see something!' cried Podgy Plum suddenly.

'Hills!' cried the Little Captain.

'And rocks!' cried Podgy Plum. 'Rocks with caves in them.'

The trail led straight to them.

'Careful, now,' said Marinka. 'The robbers are there.'

But the Little Captain rode on at full gallop. The Little Captain was not afraid, not even of forty thieves.

'*Hup!*' he himself now shouted to the camel, steering straight for the biggest and darkest cave, the cave of Borrow, Morrow and Allmysorrow.

'Hey there!' shouted the Little Captain. 'I'll get you, you nasty robbers!'

'Robbers!' came the answer, but it was only an echo. The camel stopped just at the entrance. The Little Captain and Podgy Plum jumped down. Marinka stayed where she was—she didn't like it.

'*Yoohoo!*' called Podgy Plum.

'*Hoohoohoo!*' echoed the cave.

Marinka liked it even less. 'They're waiting to ambush you,' she whispered shakily.

But the Little Captain walked inside. All he found in the half-darkness was a blackened cauldron and a single crystal rabbit which Allmysorrow had left behind.

The robbers had gone, with Timid Thomas, the camels and the treasure chests.

What now? There were so many tracks by the cave that it was impossible to see which way the robbers had gone. And Timid Thomas had not written any more.

Suddenly Marinka began to sob. 'We'll never find them again,' she wept. 'Never again.'

Podgy Plum gave the cauldron a hefty kick. The thing rolled several yards across the sand and bumped into the crystal rabbit. *Pling*! went the crystal rabbit.

'*Pling*!' said Podgy Plum furiously. He was going to kick the rabbit too, but Marinka picked it up. 'Leave it!' she cried. 'I want to keep it.'

The Little Captain was standing outside in the sand, legs planted firmly apart, staring grave-eyed towards the horizon. 'Bless my soul,' said the Little Captain, narrowing his eyes and looking again. There, just above the horizon, he saw a sparkling dream garden hanging in the air, just as Timid Thomas had done.

The Little Captain pinched himself. 'I'm not dreaming,' he muttered, 'and I'm not thirsty. And yet I can see a mirage. So it must be real. A real garden, over the horizon.'

The Little Captain was right. The garden which Timid Thomas had seen in his imagination really did exist. It was an old, deserted garden, with a tumbledown palace where an exiled sheik had once lived. And sometimes, in the heat of the day, you could see the ruins and the trees and the flowers up in the air, because hot air sometimes acts as a mirror, just like water.

'Aha,' thought the Little Captain, 'I think the robbers have gone there.'

He called Marinka and Podgy Plum and the three of them mounted the camel again, the three of them said 'Gee up!' all together and made straight for the place where they had seen the reflection in the sky.

The Little Captain had been right again. The robbers were on their way to the secret garden. But Allmysorrow did not know the place exactly, because he always rode back to front on his donkey, and Timid Thomas did not know the place at all. The camels with their heavy treasure chests trailed sluggishly through the sand and Borrow and Morrow grew more and more impatient. 'Where is it, then?' they kept crying. 'Where is it then?' And Timid Thomas pointed with a shaking finger: 'There!' But Allmysorrow would cry: 'No, no, there!' And so the robber caravan and the treasures rode across the desert in swoops and semi-circles.

But the camel carrying the Little Captain, Marinka and Podgy Plum rode in a straight line, at the gallop.

And when at last, at last, at last, the first robber, Borrow, saw something sparkling in the distance which looked like a garden, a real garden with walls and a gateway, and when, after endless jolting, they reached the beautiful golden gate, there was a camel standing there with three children on its back, barring the way.

'Halt!' they heard. 'Give back the stolen treasures! They belong with me. I am the Little Captain.'

Three More Chests

There they stood. One camel, carrying the Little Captain, Marinka and Podgy Plum, facing six camels, two horses and a donkey, with the robbers Borrow, Morrow and Allmysorrow on their backs, as well as the treasure chests and whimpering Thomas.

The golden gate of the garden which was no longer a mirage stood wide open.

'Ha, ha,' laughed Borrow. 'Are you going to stop us?'

'Choose!' laughed Morrow. 'Shall we throw you in the fountain or in the sand?'

'Look out, look out!' sang Allmysorrow. 'They'll knock you about.'

But the Little Captain looked straight into their faces.

'Robbers,' he said, 'give back the treasure. And the camels.'

'Well,' cried Borrow, 'do you mean they're yours?'

'No,' said the Little Captain, 'they are not mine. But —'

'Well, then!' laughed Borrow. His teeth flashed.

'Out of the way!' cried Morrow. His knife slashed.

'And as for you,' sang Allmysorrow, 'we'll cut you in two.'

But the Little Captain was not afraid. The Little Captain went on sitting calmly on the camel's front hump, because the Little Captain had not finished speaking. He said: 'The treasures belong to the sons of the Great Lord of Fear and Terror. That's where we're taking them.'

He might have pronounced a spell. The knife fell from Morrow's hands, Borrow's mouth fell wide open and Allmysorrow fell off his donkey.

'*What?*' cried all three robbers together. And then they shouted something else, their voices hoarse. They shouted: 'It's *Father's?*' There was a tremendous hubbub. Timid Thomas thought they were fighting and buried his face in his hands, but it was not a fight, it was a dance of joy. Borrow and Morrow leaped about on the sand like madmen. Allmysorrow billowed away on his accordion, the horses whinnied, the donkey brayed and the camels stood primly by.

Timid Thomas stopped his ears, but Marinka and Podgy Plum sat staring wide-eyed at the strange spectacle.

'Wh-what does it all mean?' asked Podgy Plum.

'It means,' said the Little Captain, 'that we have found them.'

'Who's *them?*' asked Marinka.

The Little Captain pointed to the dancing robbers. 'Those are three of the sons of the Great Lord of Fear and Terror,' he said. 'Just as I thought. They weren't real robbers at all.'

Then Marinka's mouth opened wide. 'How could you tell?' she asked.

For answer the Little Captain pulled an old, crumpled, yellowed piece of paper out of his pocket. It was the letter which had been with the treasure chests. 'Do you remember the last few lines?' he said, and he read them aloud:

> 'And as for theft, rely on me!
> A thieving hand would, through my spell,
> be clamped for ever to the wheel.'

'Scurvyboots?' asked Podgy Plum.

'Yes, Scurvyboots,' said the Little Captain. 'But it applies to other robbers too. Borrow's, Morrow's and Allmysorrow's hands would have stuck to the camels' reins if they had been robbers. But they are the sons of the Great Lord himself.'

Meanwhile the sons had gone leaping and singing and jumping through the golden gate into the garden.

'Listen,' cried Borrow. 'We're going to build this ruined palace up again, because we have gold in plenty.'

'Listen,' cried Morrow. 'We're going to live here from now on, because we have silver without end.'

'Listen,' cried Allmysorrow. 'The crystal rabbits! They pling and plong so prettily.'

'SILENCE!' ordered the Little Captain. He was standing in the middle. 'You have chosen,' he said. 'A chest each; the one filled with gold, the silver, and the crystal rabbits. Take them! The rest goes back with us, because now we shall have to go in search of the other two sons who went to the Wild West. And the only daughter, who lives in the Far North.'

'NO!' cried Timid Thomas. 'I want to go home.'

'HELP!' shrieked Timid Thomas, because Borrow suddenly picked him up and threw him through the air to Morrow, who threw him to Allmysorrow, who threw him back to Borrow. 'We'll keep you here!' they cried, laughing. 'As a gardener's boy.'

But that was a joke. After a feast under the rustling trees of the secret garden, there in the Deep South, the four children set off again on their camels with the remaining treasure chests towards the coast where the *Neversink* lay at anchor. Three long, hot days they spent on the journey, but they had enough to eat and drink and the Little Captain's brave little boat lay bobbing on the blue waves, waiting for them.

The three treasure chests were placed in the hold. Podgy Plum blew up the furnace, Marinka made some more pancake dough, Timid Thomas began to swab obediently and the Little Captain pulled the steam whistle. It was a goodbye whistle to the seven camels which had carried them so kindly and which could now wander about freely again in the desert where they felt so much at home.

The Little Captain set course for the west. The sun went down, the moon came up, and then, just before they were going to bed, all four of them at once saw a great white bird. No, not a bird. Sails. The sails of a sailing ship, the ghost ship of Scurvyboots. The old pirate was at the wheel. 'Maties!' he bellowed. 'Maties! Look!'

The Little Captain, Podgy Plum, Marinka and Timid Thomas saw him waving. Waving one arm wildly in the air, as he flew past like a phantom.

'Look at that,' muttered the Little Captain. 'We have handed over half the treasure. One arm has already been released from the spell.'

Westward Ho!

The west lies where the sun sets. You would think that there was an enormously deep pit at that spot for the sun to crawl into, so that the world turns dark. But where exactly is the pit? In a meadow, in a wood, among the mountains? Or in the sea? Of course it couldn't be in the sea. But the west must be somewhere, mustn't it?

The *Neversink* had been sailing for weeks, straight for the west. The Little Captain never once turned off course. He held the wheel in his fists without giving it a single twist, and there he stood, feet apart, eyes on the horizon, where the sun sank every day.

But the place was as far away as ever.

Marinka had used up all the flour on pancakes, Podgy Plum had put all the coal on the fire and Timid Thomas's swab had not a hair left on it. Timid Thomas had no tears left either: he had wept them all out of his eyes with sorrow, because the *Neversink* was still not going home. He was looking forward to going back to school so much!

'We'll be in the west soon, you'll see,' Marinka comforted him. But Timid Thomas didn't like the sound of that either, because it meant that they would plunge into the enormous pit, boat and all.

'We shall have to put into harbour somewhere,' said the Little Captain, 'to lay in provisions.'

'And to ask the way,' said Podgy Plum.

'And to buy fresh tears,' said Marinka, 'because Timid Thomas is drying out completely.'

The first harbour they came to was the port of Xuxuxalpetl. A little village on the bay of a forgotten coast, set among cliffs, no more than five houses and a pub. A sailors' pub.

And in the five houses lived five old sea captains who sat playing cards all day in the sailors' pub. They drank black beer with foam on top and all they said was 'Five of hearts' or 'Ace of clubs' and now and again 'Trump!'

'Trump!' one of the old sea captains was just saying, when the Little Captain in his big cap came striding in.

'Great heavens above!' all five cried together, and it was the first time for years that they had said anything but 'Five of hearts' or 'Ace of clubs'.

'Good-day all,' said the Little Captain, touching his cap politely. 'Could you please tell me where the west actually lies?'

The five old sea captains looked at each other. Then their big mouths opened all together and they began to roar with laughter. 'The west! Ho ho ho! A captain, asking for the west!' And they banged the Little Captain on the shoulder so that he almost sank through the floor; it was the best joke they had ever heard.

'Beer!' they cried. 'A mug of beer for the young captain!' And they pushed him into a chair and all five came to sit round him and poured the mug down his throat.

The Little Captain was forced to drink. He got a white moustache and a white beard from the foam and the black beer made him feel dizzy and giddy.

'Cheers!' they cried. 'Can you play cards?'

But the Little Captain could no longer tell the difference between the five of hearts and the ace of clubs. They danced before his eyes, he slumped against the table, his cap askew over his nose and with a loud yawn he fell asleep, snoring like a real, big, old sea captain.

'Heavens above...!'

The five sea captains gazed at him as if their own ships had run aground in the open sea.

'What kind of a captain is that?' asked number one.

'After only one mug!' cried number two.

'Could he have been an exhausted castaway?' asked number three.

'I wonder where he comes from?' murmured number four.

'Let's see if he's got any papers on him,' suggested number five.

They searched through his clothes. Out of the Little Captain's trouser pocket came a handkerchief, marked L.C., a pretty pink shell and a compass. Out of his back pocket came a rope's end, a rusty nail and a penny piece. Out of his jacket pocket came a bit of wire, two little wheels, a rubber and a map of the blue sea. Out of his breast pocket came a yellowing photograph. 'Could that have been his mother?' asked one of the sea captains. They were quiet for a moment, so that only the snores of the Little Captain could be heard. Then they felt in his inside pocket.

'Aha! A letter!'

They bumped into each other, put pairs of rusty steel-rimmed spectacles on their noses and began to read aloud: 'To the Great Lord of Fear and Terror,' and underneath:

> Herewith the seven chests! Each one is
> filled with treasure: crystal bunnies,
> copper, silver, rubies red,
> diamonds, bigger than your head.
> The sixth oak chest is filled with gold,
> but luck is what the seventh holds.
> I send them to you, sir, by sea,
> and as for theft, rely on me!
> A thieving hand would, through my spell,
> be clamped for ever to the wheel.'

The five sea captains took off their five rusty pairs of glasses and looked at each other.

'There's something fishy about this,' they muttered. 'This talk of treasures and robbers won't do. They're sure to want to go through the lock gates ...'

On board the *Neversink*, Podgy Plum and Marinka and Timid Thomas who were waiting for the Little Captain to come back, grew anxious.

The Little Captain had been gone a long, long time ...

Where Is the Little Captain?

When, after three whole hours, the Little Captain had still not returned, Marinka said: 'I'll go and look for him.'

All that time the three of them had been sitting waiting in the cabin of the *Neversink*, where it lay moored in the harbour of Xuxuxalpetl.

'I'll go with you,' said Podgy Plum.

Timid Thomas was already beginning to turn pale. 'Must I stay here to ɪ-look after the ship?' he asked. For Timid Thomas always had to do that.

'Of course,' said Marinka. 'And if anyone comes, just pull on the steam whistle. Once for a thief, twice for a raider and three times for the Little Captain.'

Timid Thomas tried to remember this while Marinka and Podgy Plum walked towards the little square of five houses and a pub. Timid Thomas would have liked to creep into the hold, but then he would not be able to reach the steam-whistle cord.

'Sea-folk always go to the pub first,' said Marinka firmly, and she stepped bravely into the taproom, followed by Podgy Plum.

'Great heavens above,' cried the five sea captains, 'still more children!'

'We're looking for the Little Captain,' said Marinka. 'Has he been here?'

'Been? Ho ho ho!' The sea captains roared with laughter and pointed to the floor behind the bar. There lay the Little Captain, still snoring after the black beer.

'Is he ill?' asked Marinka anxiously.

'No, no,' said Podgy Plum. 'He's tired. He's been standing at the wheel for eight days on end.'

The five sea captains looked at each other. 'Running away, I suppose?' they said. 'With all those treasures on board?'

'What?' cried Marinka. 'How did you get hold of that?'

The five sea captains showed her the old, crumpled and yellowed piece of paper that they had found in the Little Captain's inside pocket. 'It says so here,' they said.

'But hasn't the Little Captain told you what it means?' asked Marinka.

'He was asleep,' they said.

Then Marinka and Podgy Plum told the whole story: of Scurvyboots the pirate who had stolen the seven chests long ago and, as a punishment, had had to sail the seven seas on his ghost ship ever since. He could be released when the seven chests had been delivered and the Little Captain was doing that now, but the seven chests had to be taken to the children of the Great Lord of Fear and Terror, because the Great Lord himself had been dead for a long time. They told how they had handed over the first chest, full of huge diamonds, to the eldest son in the Misty East, the next three chests to the three sons who lived in the Deep South, and were now on their way to the Wild West, where two more sons had gone, and —

'The Wild West?' cried the five sea captains. 'Great heavens above! The Wild West is the Boiling Sea. Behind here.'

They pointed with their five thick thumbs through the wall of the taproom. 'Not a soul can live there.'

Marinka stiffened.

But Podgy Plum asked: 'What is the Boiling Sea, then?'

'That, young matey,' said the sea captains, 'is the most dangerous sea there is. So dangerous that it is not shown on any map. When there is a storm there, and there is a storm about three times a day, you get slam, bang and bubble waves which smash your ship to smithereens before you can count up to thirteen and suck it to the bottom.'

'Oh,' said Marinka. 'But the Little Captain is not afraid of anything.'

'Well, well,' said the five.

'And our boat, the *Neversink*, can stand up to a few knocks,' said Podgy Plum.

'Well, well,' said the five. 'Then we had better tell you that there is only one vessel in existence which can sail the Boiling Sea. A ship as big as a town. It comes here just once a year, and that ship is the only one we ever allow through the lock.'

'Through the lock?' asked Podgy Plum. 'Is there a lock here?'

'You bet your life, what did you think? That you could just sail into the Boiling Sea? They made a fine watergate for it. And we look after it.'

'Oh,' said Marinka, 'so the *Neversink* ...' Then she had an idea: 'This once-a-year ship, when will it be coming again?'

'Just been,' said the five sea captains. 'Two days back.'

Podgy Plum and Marinka stared at the ground. What were they to do? How would they ever get into the Boiling Sea, and still worse: would they be able to find the two sons there? After all, if no one could live there ...

'Little Captain!' cried Marinka, and she ran to the bar to shake him awake.

But the Little Captain was not lying behind the bar; he was not in the taproom at all. The Little Captain had gone.

'Eh?' said Marinka.

But Podgy Plum raised a finger. 'Listen!'

In the distance they heard the *Neversink's* steam whistle. Three shrill notes.

'He's back on board! Come on!'

But when Marinka and Podgy Plum rushed up the gangplank, the only person they met was a pale Thomas.

'Th-thieves,' stammered Thomas, 'I thought I heard thieves. Th-th-three thieves.'

There was no one to be seen, not even the Little Captain. Where was the Little Captain?

The Boiling Sea

The Little Captain had
woken up behind the
bar while Marinka and
Podgy Plum were talking to
the five sea captains. He had heard all about the Boiling
Sea, and about the ship as big as a town and about the
lock gate.

'The lock gate!' thought the Little Captain and like a
mouse he stole out of the back door of the taproom. 'If
I can open the lock gate,' thought the Little Captain, 'I
shall sail through it with the *Neversink*.' For the Little
Captain was determined to get to the Wild West, even if
there was a Boiling Sea in which every ship was wrecked.
The *Neversink* was not called 'never sink' for nothing.

The lock gate lay at the end of the little sea port and
in order to open it you had to turn a wheel. It was heavy
work and it squeaked, but the Little Captain strained and
sweated until the big watergate stood ajar, wide enough
to let the *Neversink* through.

Then the Little Captain ran back to the quay where
his boat was moored. He had heard the steam whistle

blow three times and he realized that the others were on board and growing anxious.

'Here I am,' he cried, jumping on deck. 'Quick, anchor aweigh. Full steam ahead.'

'But Little Captain!' cried Marinka. 'Where —'

'Sssh,' said the Little Captain, grasping the helm.

'Little Captain,' cried Podgy Plum, 'there's nowhere —'

'Sssh,' said the Little Captain, steering out of the harbour.

'Little Captain!' screeched Timid Thomas. 'We're not going, not going to...' For Timid Thomas had been hearing all the tales of the Boiling Sea.

But the Little Captain nodded. 'We're going,' he said, and he steered straight for the open lock gate.

The five old sea captains were about to start playing cards again when they heard the little boat leaving. They glanced out of the window and waved their arms. 'Goodbye,' they muttered, and then their arms stiffened in the air. 'Great heavens above!' they cried. 'He's sailing for the lock!'

As one man, they rushed out of the door. 'Hey, halt, stop!' they roared to the *Neversink*. 'Close the lock gate,' they told each other.

The *Neversink* sped through the water under full power.

The five sea captains flew puffing along the quay.

The *Neversink* reached the lock first.

As the sea captains began to turn the wheel to close the lock gate, the little boat just slipped through the narrow gap and the foaming water spattered the faces of the sea captains.

'You're mad!' they roared. 'Little madcap, you're as mad as a hatter!'

For answer came the piercing shriek of the steam whistle as the Little Captain tugged it and then the piercing screech of Timid Thomas, as he saw the Boiling Sea opening up ahead of him.

'Great heavens above,' muttered the five big sea captains, 'that crazy clown is heading straight for disaster,' and they stared in silence at the doughty little boat, until they had to put their five pairs of rusty steel glasses back on their noses, it had grown so small.

The *Neversink* sailed bravely on. The waves were calm—no slam, bang or bubble; the Boiling Sea was still, for the wind was having a day of rest.

Timid Thomas had fled to the hold and was sitting there in the seventh chest, the empty good-luck chest, which seemed to him the safest place.

Marinka and Podgy Plum were standing by the wheel, looking pale.

'Little Captain,' Marinka began, 'you do know that every ship is wrecked when there's a storm here?'

'Yes,' said the Little Captain.

'Little Captain,' said Podgy Plum, 'wouldn't it be better for us to wait for the ship as big as a town and cross the sea on that?'

'No,' said the Little Captain.

The colour of the water was dark grey, because the Boiling Sea was thirteen fathoms deep. And the coast was a high wall of steep cliffs, for the Boiling Sea was in the shape of an enormous saucepan half full of water.

The Little Captain tugged at the steam whistle and the echo travelled to and fro thirteen times, from one rocky shore to another and back again.

'They must have heard that,' he said, 'so they will come out by themselves.'

'Who?'

'The sons, of course. The two sons of the Great Lord of Fear and Terror. They must be somewhere here.'

Every quarter of an hour the Little Captain blew the whistle, but nothing appeared and so they sailed on, hour after hour, until dusk began to fall.

And then—'Listen!' cried Podgy Plum—it seemed as if there was an answer. Another steam whistle, far away in the distance. At the same moment all three of them saw it, faintly, on the horizon: houses, roofs, towers, windmills.

'A town!' shouted Marinka.

'How can that be?' cried Podgy Plum.

The Little Captain said: 'It's the ship. It's a floating town.'

'Where, where?' asked Timid Thomas, who had bounced up out of the hold with relief.

But Timid Thomas saw nothing, because it was suddenly dark. Not because the sun had gone down, but because clouds had blown up, pitch-black clouds, ink-black clouds.

Storm clouds ...

The Storm

The five sea captains had been playing cards in their inn for a long time when the storm burst.

'Eight of clubs,' said one. 'Wind force ten.'

'Ten of clubs,' said another. 'Wind force twelve.'

'Trump!' cried the third. 'It's a hurricane.'

And a hurricane it was. The wind flung itself, howling, on the roofs of Xuxuxalpetl, blew the roof tiles through the air like fluttering leaves and smashed the chimneys on the streets below. 'Jack of diamonds,' said the fourth sea captain. 'It's a roaring hurricane.'

'Ace of diamonds!' cried the fifth sea captain. But at that moment all the playing cards were blown off the table by the wind which came whistle-sissling in round the windows. 'Good heavens above!'

The sea captains had never known anything like this storm. The water in the harbour sploshed over the quay and licked at the doorsteps with its long tongues of foam.

'It will be tremendously rough out there,' the five sea captains thought, 'out on the Boiling Sea,' and they thought of the little madcap, sitting in the midst of it on his little boat.

'It will be lying on the bottom like a bit of crumpled lead,' they told each other and they would have taken their caps off, but the caps had already been blown off by the wind, and all five were flying through the air like black stormy petrels.

There was no need for the five sea captains to take their caps off anyway, for the *Neversink* was not sunk yet.

True, the six-bucket funnel had been blown overboard in six rattling pieces, the mast had been carried off in forty-seven splinters, the furled sail had flown away in tatters with the driving clouds and the roof of the cabin was being banged open and shut like a lid by the churning winds, but the little boat was afloat.

It was tossed to and fro like a cork, but however hard the seething waves tried to bruise it or break it or suck

it into the whirling depths, the little boat stayed whole and it stayed afloat.

It was the *Neversink*.

And the crew?

The deck was swept clean, there was no one there. The cabin was full of water, the helm was spinning madly and the place behind the helm was empty. Where was the Little Captain?

The Little Captain was in the hold. All four of them were sitting in the hold and the hatch was firmly bolted. At the first squall of wind the Little Captain had given the order immediately: 'Get below. Batten down the hatch.'

And there they sat. Or rather, there they rolled and bowled and bashed and crashed to and fro. No one knew which arms and legs belonged to whom any more, no

one really knew who they were. One lump of misery had once been Timid Thomas, another Marinka and the larger lump of misery was probably Podgy Plum. Only the Little Captain was still capable of thought.

'The coast,' thought the Little Captain, 'the high, steep, hard rocky cliffs. If we're being driven towards that we shall be smashed to smithereens. Then everything will be lost, my boat, the three treasure chests and the four of us. And Scurvyboots, too.'

The Little Captain listened to the wind which rushed howling along the iron hull of his boat and to the waves which sounded like thunderous hammer blows.

Hour after hour passed by. Was it day by now? Not a glimmer of light fell into the hold and it was beginning to feel close.

Then the Little Captain thought of the chest, the seventh, lucky chest which they had with them in the hold. 'Shall we crawl inside?' he wondered. 'Would the chest —'

But at that moment there came a terrible groaning and cracking and creaking of iron. A shock ran through the *Neversink*, the worst they had yet known, and then the boat lay still. As still as a dead bird.

'The rocks!' That was the first thought that went through the Little Captain's head when he recovered from the stunning blow. 'We have hit the cliffs. At the top, I should think.'

But could the *Neversink* possibly have been lifted *that* high by the waves?

'W-where am I?' came Marinka's voice.

'Ooh,' stammered Podgy Plum, 'what a ghastly dream I had.'

'It was no dream,' said the Little Captain.

'Si-si-sick ... oooh!' Timid Thomas could be heard. 'So sick...'

The Little Captain said: 'The *Neversink* has been washed up on the rocks. We must try to open the hatch.'

But they had not the strength to do it. The screws had been bent by the might of the waves.

'Bother,' said Podgy Plum.

'What do we do now?' asked Marinka.

'I want to go home!' moaned Timid Thomas.

But the Little Captain said: 'Wait calmly.'

And the Little Captain said something else. He said: 'It's a funny thing, it feels as if we were still moving ...'

The Floating Town

The floating town, the incredibly vast ship which crossed the Boiling Sea once a year, was not bothered by the storm. Although the slam-bang and bubble waves did their best, the ship's hull did not bend by a millimetre. And although the hurricane winds lashed and tore at roofs and chimneys, everything remained immovable.

The ship sailed calmly on, with scarcely so much as a roll.

It was a strange vessel, because the deck consisted of streets and houses, towers and windmills, a church and a tiny little white palace.

A hundred people lived in the floating town and all hundred of them slept like logs on the night of the storm.

'Brisk little blow,' they said. 'Sleep well, now!'

Only the people at the wheel had stayed up, because of course they had to steer. They steered straight for the west. When in the middle of the night they heard the sound of a heavy thud, they scarcely looked up. Just an extra-big wave, they thought.

Those few who woke up because the thud was so close to their houses, muttered: 'A storm, eh?', yawned, turned over comfortably and went on sleeping.

But next morning they rubbed their eyes in astonishment, for there, in the little square outside their windows, lay a boat. A real boat, dumped down by a huge wave.

'We've never seen the likes of that before,' cried the people of the floating town, running outside to look. What a sad little wreck! No mast, no funnel, the cabin roofless and half filled with water.

'Poor shipwrecked souls,' said one.

'Their own silly fault,' said another.

'I say,' began a third, looking pale, 'wasn't that—wasn't it yesterday evening when we heard a steam whistle? Could it be —'

'Oh yes,' said a fourth, 'that must have been this little ship. Poor —'

All of them began taking off their hats. They were not blown away, because the storm had died down.

'Look, it's called the *Neversink*,' said one.

'*Pile-of-junk* would suit it better now,' said another.

'Get some pincers,' said a third. He wanted to try to unscrew the hatch. 'There might be something inside.'

'Yes,' said a joker, 'sea water.'

The pincers did not work, because the screws were bent. But at last they managed to open the hold with a hatchet. And then the people of the floating town drew back in fright.

From the opening of the hold rose a ghost. A ghastly face, with a mop of hair, whimpering hollowly: 'Si-si-sick.'

The face vanished, there was the sound of clattering

and thumping from the hold of the little boat and once again a head appeared. It shouted: 'Ahoy!'

It was not a ghost, it was a little girl who came crawling out, jumped down from the deck and asked: 'Where are we?'

The people of the floating town were speechless. At last: 'Th-then you're not drowned?' they asked.

'Of course not,' cried Marinka, and 'What did you think?' cried Podgy Plum behind her.

'We are!' moaned Timid Thomas, sticking his pale, ghostly face out again. 'We're shipwrecked.'

'Och, puir wee thing,' cried a woman's voice. 'Such a wee loon on a big voyage.' But then her mouth fell open wide, all their mouths fell open wide, for the Little Captain had just appeared, and he too seemed to be just a little fellow.

'Maircy on us!' cried the woman. 'What kind of a wee boat is that? A bairns' boat?'

But the little fellow stood there in his big cap, feet set apart on the sloping deck, and spoke: 'I am the Little Captain and this is my ship, the *Neversink*. We were overtaken by a storm and have suffered damage. Take us to your captain to discuss the matter.'

Five minutes later they were sitting in the little white palace on the floating town, in comfortable chairs with fat cushions and hot coffee and thick sandwiches on the table in front of them. All but Timid Thomas, for he had been tucked up in bed with three hot water bottles and given weak tea and a biscuit.

'Well, well,' said the steward of the floating town, 'how about some more coffee? And tell us, where were you headed for?'

'The west,' said the Little Captain.

'Well, that's all right!' cried the steward. 'That's the way we're going. Always westward, for years and years and years.'

'What?' asked Marinka. 'For years? Is it such a long way off?'

'Oh, lassie,' said the steward, 'we've been at least seven times round the world. Always sailing westward.'

'But—but—' Podgy Plum began, 'then how can we ever—I mean we're looking—somewhere in the Wild West —'

Before Podgy Plum could go on, the door opened and the captain appeared. And then another captain. For the floating town was so big that two captains were needed to command it.

'Aha,' they said. 'Welcome, castaways.'

They put out their hands. 'May we introduce ourselves? My name is Fear, and this is my brother Terror.'

The Little Captain looked as if he had been struck by lightning.

'Ha ha!' they laughed. 'Don't be afraid! They're just names. That was our father's name: he was the Great Lord of Fear and Terror ...'

Five Captains

Marinka was the first to be able to speak.

'Captain Fear!' she cried. 'Captain Terror!' She jumped up and flung herself on their necks, with so many kisses that the caps rolled off their heads.

'Well, well, she's not frightened,' said the captains, with scarlet cheeks.

'She's glad to have been rescued, of course,' said the steward.

'Oh no,' said Podgy Plum. 'Marinka is glad that we've found them.'

'Them? What *them?*'

'You tell them, Little Captain,' said Podgy Plum.

The Little Captain stood with his feet planted firmly apart, looked straight at the big captains and spoke: 'We were searching for the two sons of the Great Lord of Fear and Terror.'

Now it was their turn to stand speechless and open-mouthed.

'Yes,' the Little Captain continued, 'because we have a chest for each of you. One filled with copper and one filled with red rubies.'

'W-what?'

'That's right,' the Little Captain continued. 'We had seven chests for your father. But since he is no longer alive, we have had to take them round to his sons. One in the Misty East, three in the Deep South, two here in the Wild West and the last, the chest filled with good luck, we shall now have to take to your sister in the Far North.'

And the Little Captain told them all about Scurvyboots the pirate, who must be released from his ghost ship, and about the adventures they had been through.

The brothers Fear and Terror looked at each other. 'Two treasure chests,' they murmured. 'Now we can buy an engine for our tub. No one will have to row any more.'

'Row?' asked Marinka.

Podgy Plum began to laugh. 'This isn't a fairground boat, is it?' he asked.

'It's an ancient galley,' said the brothers Fear and Terror. And then they told their story. How after the death of their father they had left the country to travel west. How they had bought this vessel with the last of their money in order to be able to take the hundred faithful subjects who wanted to stay with them. How they had rowed, with fifty people at a time, on the heavy sweeps, always following the setting sun. How they had become desperate because the west never came any nearer, how in the end they had become resigned and built a town on their vessel to live in. And how they still went on rowing, in their floating town, to the west, always to the west ...

'But now,' they cried, 'now we shall buy a big steam engine and a propeller. Then the ship will move by itself, and faster, too.'

At the end of the Boiling Sea there was another narrow channel and they passed through it into the blue ocean. On the coast lay a big port where the steam engine was built into the floating town. It was fitted with two propellers and five rudders as well.

'It's necessary,' they said, 'otherwise we shan't be able to steer the thing. You need five captains for it.'

The brothers Fear and Terror scratched their heads, but the Little Captain said: 'In Xuxuxalpetl there are five sea captains. They can do it.'

That was a good idea. After the *Neversink* had been repaired, with a brand-new six-bucket funnel, a proud mast made of pine wood, a fine, strong sail and a new roof on the cabin, the floating town sailed away. First towards the east, back across the Boiling Sea, with the five wheels side by side in the wheelhouse manned by the brothers Fear and Terror, Podgy Plum, Marinka and the Little Captain. Timid Thomas did not dare.

Timid Thomas wandered all day along the streets and past the houses of the floating town and whenever clouds appeared in the sky he fled indoors.

'Come for a snack, little chap?' the women of the floating town would ask. And Timid Thomas nodded, because he dared not say that he was frightened of a storm.

But no storm came during their passage. The *Neversink* could have sailed by itself instead of standing on the deck of the floating town.

So they reached Xuxuxalpetl, where the five sea captains had just started quarrelling over their cards.

'Ace of hearts—ace of spades—ace of hearts—ace of spades!' they were shouting at each other. But when they heard that all five of them could be captains of a ship at once, they cried: 'Trumps! We'll do it!'

So the floating town has been sailing across the sea from that day to this, always westward, trying to overtake the setting sun.

But the *Neversink* sailed northwards, to search for the last heir of the Great Lord of Fear and Terror, his youngest daughter. For the seventh chest, the chest filled with luck, was for her.

'But it's empty!' whimpered Timid Thomas. 'Let's go home now.'

But the Little Captain sailed straight ahead, heading for the North Pole, steady and sure behind the helm, his eyes on the horizon.

The Old Watchman

The world is so big, so big. There is more sea than land in the world. The sea is blue, or grey, but far, far to the north the sea is green. White blocks of ice float in it, as big as mountains, and it is dangerous to sail between them in a boat.

And yet a little boat was sailing over the green sea in the Far North. It had a funnel made of six buckets and the steam furnace was an upturned bathtub. At the helm a little captain stood, steering round the icebergs. In front of the furnace a podgy lad knelt, blowing up the fire. In the galley a girl stood stirring pancake mixture. On the afterdeck a shivering little boy went round with a swab and a pail. His fingers were red with cold.

The last land lies up there in the Far North. It is made of black rock and on the last point of it stands a tall lighthouse. In it lives the Old Watchman, making the northern lights, which shine in the polar night with red and yellow and green and sometimes with blue flames.

The Old Watchman is lonely and he was very pleased when he saw the little boat sailing towards him, making for the jetty to come alongside. He ran down all the stairs, the iron staircase with its six hundred and fourteen steps, and opened the lighthouse door.

'Well, well,' he said, for there were four children standing in front of him.

'I am the Little Captain,' said the first, 'of the steamship *Neversink*, and this is my crew: Podgy Plum, Marinka and Timid Thomas.'

'Well, well,' said the Old Watchman again.

'May we come in?' asked the Little Captain.

They walked up the six hundred and fourteen iron stairs to the little room at the top, where a stove was roaring.

The Little Captain took off his cap and Timid Thomas warmed his red fingers.

'Are you lost?' asked the Old Watchman.

'No,' said the Little Captain, 'we're on a search.'

'For polar bears?' asked the Old Watchman. 'Or for whales?'

'For a noble lady,' said the Little Captain.

'Well, well.'

'Have you heard of her?' asked the Little Captain.

The Old Watchman scratched his grey head. 'The Noble Lady of the Far North lives in the ice citadel on top of the slippery Slitherberg,' he said. 'What do you want with her?'

'We've got a present for her,' said the Little Captain. 'A chest full of good luck.'

The Old Watchman did not laugh. 'Ah,' he said, 'that would do her good. The Noble Lady of the Far North is a sad lady. But a chest! You'll never get a chest up the slippery Slitherberg. You won't be able to get up it yourselves. No one can get up.'

'Perhaps the Noble Lady would come down?' asked the Little Captain.

The Old Watchman shook his head. 'Never,' he said.

'We'll go and try, all the same,' said the Little Captain. 'It's for the pirate Scurvyboots.'

'Is he in the chest?' asked the watchman anxiously.

'No,' said the Little Captain. 'The pirate Scurvyboots is sailing round on his ghost ship with his hands fixed to the wheel by a spell. It's a punishment, because he stole the seven chests full of treasure. We've taken six chests back and one of Scurvyboots' hands is already free. The seventh chest is for the Noble Lady. She's the daughter of the Great Lord of Fear and Terror, for whom the treasure was meant.'

The Old Watchman scratched his grey head again. 'Scurvyboots,' he muttered, 'that's another sorry business.'

The Little Captain asked: 'Where does the ice castle lie?'

'No!' cried Timid Thomas suddenly. He sat shivering beside the hot stove.

'He's so cold,' said Marinka. 'Have you got a pullover for him?'

'I've got pullovers for you all,' said the Old Watchman. 'I've got furry suits for you. If you are really going to the icy citadel on the slippery Slitherberg you will have to wear polar outfits.'

Polar outfits are the warmest clothes in the world, with fur on the inside. Podgy Plum was as round as a barrel when he put his on. Marinka thought the colour was dull and the Little Captain put his cap on top of his fur hood. It fitted properly at last. The Old Watchman showed them the way to go. 'It's three days' sail,' he said. 'Look out for icebergs and for polar bears.'

The Little Captain thanked him and was about to set off down the six hundred and fourteen iron steps again, but the Old Watchman said: 'I have something else for you.'

From a little box he took two sticks with a knob on the end and gave them to the Little Captain. 'These are signal rockets,' he said. 'This one gives a green light—set it off if things are going well. But this one gives a red light—set it off if you are in danger. Farewell!'

A quarter of an hour later the steam whistle on the *Neversink* shrilled until it echoed from the icebergs and with a foaming wake, the brave little boat sailed off across the green sea. Further, ever further towards the Far North, in the direction of the white ice castle on the slippery Slitherberg, which no one, since the lady, had yet been able to climb.

Northern Lights

After three days' sailing
the *Neversink* was so far to
the north that the sun could
only be seen suspended in the
distance like a red balloon, just
above the horizon. The light was
dim, as if it were evening all day
long, and in that half-light the icebergs looked ghostly.
Only towards midnight did the red sun dip behind the
horizon and complete darkness fall. It was a short night.
Then the Little Captain stopped the *Neversink*, and the
four children went off to sleep in their hammocks.

They had strange dreams.

The Little Captain dreamed of a mysteriously beautiful woman in a mysteriously beautiful castle. She was
very sweet and very sad.

Podgy Plum dreamed of polar bears chasing him,
panting and snuffling. He ran away, but the ground was
so slippery that he never got any further.

Marinka dreamed of a rumbustious pirate flying
through the air like a bird, but he had no wings.

Timid Thomas dreamed of green light, which glittered so dazzlingly in his eyes that it woke him up. How can that be? thought Thomas. It's pitch dark, isn't it?

He slipped out of his hammock and climbed sleepily through the hatch on deck. The night was still as death, the Pole Star shining almost directly above Timid Thomas's head.

Then, suddenly, a strange light flickered across the sky. Green light, yellow light, red light. It swelled and died like candlelight, shaping strange, magical figures, so that Timid Thomas could only think that his dream was still going on.

He stared open-mouthed at the icebergs, in which all the colours were dazzlingly reflected, and suddenly he saw the White Citadel straight ahead. High on a mountain top, with sides as smooth as glass, the citadel lay sparkling in the enchanted light. Walls, towers, pinnacles and battlements, and even the doors, were made of clear ice.

'There!' cried Timid Thomas. 'There, there!' He pointed with both hands, stretching forward as far as possible over the iron railing.

That was how they found him next morning, stiff as a sleepwalker.

Timid Thomas was woken up with hot coffee. 'Dream,' he stammered, 'lovely dream.' But when he told them about the Citadel, Marinka said: 'It must be another mirage.'

The Little Captain shook his head. 'Northern lights,' he said. 'They are real,' and he steered the *Neversink* in the direction towards which Timid Thomas had been pointing.

The passage between the icebergs grew narrower and narrower, and the *Neversink* might easily have been crushed. But the Little Captain sailed boldly on, blowing the steam whistle as he went. 'To scare off the polar bears,' he said.

'P-p-polar b-b-b-?' Timid Thomas could not even get the word to cross his lips, but he was shuddering with cold, too.

'I haven't seen a single one yet,' said Podgy Plum calmly.

'Full speed ahead!' cried the Little Captain suddenly.

They had entered a narrow channel and it looked as if the two icebergs were drifting closer and closer to each other. The passage was shrinking rapidly.

'Double power!' cried the Little Captain. 'Keep stoking up that furnace!'

Podgy Plum blew out his cheeks until he was as red as a lobster, Marinka rowed with the cooking spoon, Timid Thomas with the swab, but the passage grew narrower and narrower.

'Help!' screamed Timid Thomas. 'We shall be crushed.'

The Little Captain tugged at the steam whistle.

'Help!' shrieked Timid Thomas. 'We shall be eaten up.'

But there were no polar bears to be seen.

There was a block of ice—a huge block of ice which had been wobbling on the slope of the iceberg for years and now lost its balance, because of the vibrant shriek of the steam whistle. Rumblecumtumble, down it shot, making straight for the little boat.

But—perhaps the good-luck chest on board had something to do with it—at the last moment the block turned aside and, instead of landing with a crash on the *Neversink*, it landed with a splash in the water behind the *Neversink*. It made an enormous wave and just as the little boat was about to be stuck fast between the walls of ice it was picked up by the wave and thrust forward into a patch of open sea.

The Little Captain removed his cap.

Podgy Plum stayed where he was, kneeling in front of the furnace.

Marinka began to giggle: the whole of her fur jacket was soaked from the splash, she cried.

Timid Thomas stuck his head out of the hold and shouted: 'There, there, there!'

They all looked. There lay the White Citadel.

Thomas's dream had not been a dream. The slippery Slitherberg was really there, rising out of the green sea, cold, hard and shiny, like a looking-glass. The White Citadel, right at the top, looked as far out of reach as the moon.

The Signal Rocket

Three times the *Neversink* sailed slowly round the slippery Slitherberg. But the slopes were all made of ice. Not a bough, not a brick, not a boulder stuck out anywhere, there were no stairs to be seen, nor even a rope—everything was of the slipperiest ice, without a single handhold.

The Little Captain sounded the steam whistle from time to time, but no window, no doorway in the White Citadel opened and nobody appeared on the battlements. The great doors remained tight shut; there was not a sign of life to be seen.

'I bet the Noble Lady is frozen fast to her chair,' said Podgy Plum.

'She may not even be at home,' said Marinka.

But the Little Captain turned off the engine and let the *Neversink* drift gently towards the foot of the mountain.

There was no mooring jetty, but the foot of the mountain was flat. You could walk a little way, to the beginning of the smooth slope.

The Little Captain cast anchor and Podgy Plum jumped ashore. 'There seems to be a path here,' he cried. 'It runs right the way round the mountain!'

Podgy Plum began to run straight for the slope, but he got no further than a step or two. Then he slipped backwards like a struggling seal in his thick polar clothes. 'No good!' he cried.

But the Little Captain brought the seventh chest up from the hold of the *Neversink*, the last chest they had to deliver, the chest full of luck. He set it down on shore.

'And now?' asked Marinka.

'It's got to go up,' said the Little Captain.

Marinka thought it was ridiculous. 'The thing is empty,' she said. 'Leave it here, Little Captain, won't that do?'

'No,' said the Little Captain. 'It has to go to the Noble Lady in the White Citadel. Up there.'

'An empty chest!' Podgy Plum thought it was crazy, too. 'Let's turn back again,' he said. 'I bet you there's not a soul living in the whole Citadel, let alone a sorrowful lady. Bah!'

The Little Captain did not answer. The Little Captain stooped and began to push the chest forward like a sledge across the ice. He began to push it up the slope and his feet began to slip. Skid-skid on the smooth ice—he got no higher, but he went on pushing and pushing.

Marinka could not bear to watch any longer. She ran across to him and pushed as well, pushing the Little

Captain himself from behind. 'I can't leave him in the lurch now,' she thought, 'even if it's all mad.'

The chest moved up a little.

Podgy Plum looked at their struggling legs, skid-skid on the smooth ice. 'The Little Captain,' he thought, 'the Little Captain has gone round the bend.' But even as he thought, Podgy Plum took a run, bumped into Marinka so that she jerked forward, and he began to push too, skid-skid over the smooth ice.

The chest moved up a little further.

'Timid Thomas,' called Plum, 'help us!'

But Timid Thomas was still on the *Neversink*. He did not dare to come ashore.

'Come on, Thomas!' cried Podgy Plum. 'Don't be so scared. There's no danger here!'

Skid-skid went their feet over the ice and finally Podgy Plum heard a panting and snuffling behind him. Timid Thomas had found enough courage, after all, he thought to himself.

'Forward, shove!'

But instead of hands on his back, Podgy Plum felt a wet nose on his neck.

He looked round.

It was not Timid Thomas. It was a polar bear. A live one.

Podgy Plum gave a yell. He did the only thing he could do: he redoubled his efforts and ran so hard on his skidding feet that Marinka, the Little Captain and the lucky chest rose another two and a half metres up the slope.

'Well done, Plum!' shouted Marinka, and she looked around too. 'A polar bear!' yelled Marinka, and she and the Little Captain also redoubled their efforts, which took them another whole metre further up.

The polar bear was just unable to reach them.

There they were, a little way up the smooth slope of the slippery Slitherberg, running and skidding and running for their lives. It was like a nightmare in which you cannot move a step forward. How long could they keep it up?

'Timid Thomas!' they screamed. 'Chase him away!'

As if Timid Thomas would dare! Pale as a corpse, he stood watching, as if nailed to the deck of the *Neversink*, too frightened even to scream.

But then, suddenly, Timid Thomas thought of the two signal rockets which the Old Watchman on the lighthouse had given them. The green one if things were going well and the red for an emergency. And suddenly Timid Thomas went into action. Trembling, quaking and quivering, he went looking for the sticks with the knobs on, and found them at last in the cabin. 'I need the red one, I need the red one,' babbled Thomas. 'This one!' He stuck the stick in a bottle on the afterdeck, lit a match, and another, and another, until at last he was holding a flickering flame to the fuse.

Hissing, the rocket shot up into the dusky polar night and illuminated the icy scene of the slopes of the slippery Slitherberg in a fierce light.

Green light.

Timid Thomas had set off the wrong rocket.

He had used the last match.

The Old Watchman, who saw the light from his distant lighthouse, murmured contentedly: 'Aha, so everything is all right.'

But there was someone else who noticed the safe, green colour with satisfaction. Someone at sea ...

The Lucky Chest

For weeks and weeks on end the pirate Scurvyboots had been steering his ghost ship with only one hand. His other hand had been released from the spell and he did not dare to touch the helm with his free hand again. The wind had driven his ship towards the Far North and Scurvyboots was navigating with great difficulty among the icebergs, always with only one hand on the wheel.

'That's luck!' thought the pirate, when the green light of a rocket flashed before his eyes in the dusk. 'There's a safe stretch of open water.'

He made straight for it at full speed.

'For here and yonder!' shouted the pirate, and then gripped the wheel in both hands, for suddenly the slippery Slitherberg reared up ahead of him. He wrenched fiercely at the wheel, but it was too late. With a deafening crash his wooden ship rammed the iceberg, close to the place where the *Neversink* lay. Masts under full sail snapped like reeds and the bows finished up amidships, but the steering wheel was finally torn off and sailed, with the pirate held fast to it by magic, at full speed through the air.

'Help! A shipwreck!' yelled Timid Thomas from the deck of the *Neversink*.

The Little Captain, Marinka and Podgy Plum, who were still trying to make their way further up the icy slope with skidding feet, drew breath in relief. For the polar bear, which had been waiting, jaws agape, for them to slip down again, fled from the noise of the shipwreck in one great leap.

The Little Captain had just been thinking that they would have to try to crawl inside the lucky chest before the polar bear snapped them up. He had already opened the lid, but now it was no longer necessary.

Or was it?

A lucky chest is not a lucky chest for nothing, for lo and behold: the pirate Scurvyboots, who came sailing through the air at that very moment, plumped straight into it. As if into open jaws, with the wheel still in his hands, and still at full speed. At such speed that the chest, with the pirate inside, and the Little Captain, Marinka and Podgy Plum behind it, zoomed up the slopes of the slippery Slitherberg and shot straight in through the icy doors of the White Citadel.

Timid Thomas was left behind alone, down on the deck of the *Neversink*, and Timid Thomas at once began to cry because they had left him in the lurch, all alone in the dark polar night, with polar bears lying in wait for him and an abandoned ghost ship beside him. 'Boo-hoo!' howled Timid Thomas.

'*Hoo*!' The sound came back from the White Citadel. But it was not the voice of Timid Thomas. It was the voice of the sorrowful lady.

Dazed and bemused, the three children looked round, but there was no one to be seen. They could see only walls, made of ice. A ceiling, made of ice. Arches, pillars, buttresses, all ice. Tables, chairs, benches, all of ice. And at the end of the hall a wide staircase, of hard, smooth, glistening ice.

'Chilly,' said Marinka.

'Cool and cold,' said Podgy Plum.

'We must look for her,' said the Little Captain.

The pirate Scurvyboots said nothing. He saw nothing, either. The pirate Scurvyboots lay unconscious in the chest.

'He must go away,' said Marinka.

'He doesn't belong here,' said Podgy Plum

But the Little Captain shut the lid.

And at that moment, from the top of the stairs, they heard a sad song:

> 'I am the Lady of the North,
> but all the knights who come to woo
> by cold and ice are driven forth
> and splash back in the sea, boo-hoo!
> And now I think I'll never see
> a courtier come to rescue me.
> Boo-hoo, oo-hoo, how smooth the ice!

Boo-hoo, oo-hoo, it would be nice
to have a path: *one* would suffice!'

Slowly she came down the stairs, the sad lady, with a
flickering candle in her hand. She looked like a ghost.

'Ahoy,' said the Little Captain.

Giving no answer, she descended the icy stairs without
slipping once and came slowly towards them. She might
have been sleepwalking.

'Ah, why?' she sang. 'It always seems,
saviours come only in my dreams.'

'It's not a dream!' Marinka cried in a clear voice. 'We're real!'

But the Little Captain took the Noble Lady by the
hand and led her towards the chest.

'Sorrowful lady,' he said, 'we have brought this with us.
It is the seventh chest, and filled with luck. It is for you.'

'This is really too silly for words,' cried Podgy Plum.
'You can't do that, Little Captain, after all it's got —'

Podgy Plum got no further.

With a crash the lid flew open, and snorting as if he
had risen from the water, Scurvyboots the pirate rose up
from the chest. 'For here and yonder!' he bellowed, still
clutching the wheel of his ghost ship. 'Astern! Full speed
astern. We are sinking! We —'

Then he saw the Noble Lady, and the Noble Lady
saw him.

344

They gazed deep into one another's eyes and fell in love at a stroke, the pirate and the Noble Lady, and then the wheel clattered to the ground from his hands, and the candle from hers.

Scurvyboots was released from the spell.

The Noble Lady of the Far North had found her luck.

A Party in the Citadel

The White Citadel was lighted with a thousand candles and wooden steps ran from the doors to the foot of the slippery Slitherberg. Seventy-two steps, made out of the wrecked wood of the ghost ship. The *Neversink* was moored to the bottom-most step, but there was another ship there too. A gigantic ship. The floating town.

With its five sea captains, the floating town had sailed around the world, from the Wild West past the Deep South and the Misty East, until it arrived here in the Far North. All the sons of the Great Lord of Fear and Terror had come along, and now they were giving a party, up there in the White Citadel. For the marriage of their sister to Scurvyboots, who was no longer a pirate, was being celebrated, and she was now known as the Joyful Lady.

'Yoho!' cried Lord Fear.

'Och aye!' cried Lord Terror.

'Rumblecumtumble hurrah!' cried Borrow and Morrow.

'Pling!' went Allmysorrow.

'Yes, yes, well,' even the Lord of Quake and Quiver nodded. He was sitting on a chair. He was not dancing. The ice floor was too slippery for him.

'Great heavens above!' thundered the five sea captains, going off to play cards happily in a corner.

Podgy Plum and Marinka twirled, slipping and sliding, through the hall and Timid Thomas had dressed up as a polar bear so that he wouldn't need to be frightened of anyone.

In the end they all danced round the bridal pair, who sat in the middle, on the lucky chest.

'Hurrah!' came the shouts.

'Hurrah for the Little Captain!' they shouted. 'The Little Captain has saved us all!'

They wanted to drink to him, but where was the Little Captain? Not in the ballroom, not in the corridors, not in the cellar, not upstairs.

The Little Captain was standing outside, looking at the stars. At the Pole Star above his head, at the Great Bear, at the silvery Swan and at the red eye of the Bull. At the seven twinkling Pleiades, at the Whale and at the Dragon's swishing tail.

'Little Captain,' called the Noble Lady, 'what are you doing out there?'

'Noble Lady,' the Little Captain answered, 'I am seeing where I have to go.'

'Won't you stay with us?' the lady asked. 'I will be your mother.'

'Do, do!' cried Scurvyboots, beaming. 'I'll be your father.'

But the Little Captain shook his head.

'Where is your home then, Little Captain?' asked the lady.

The Little Captain stretched out his arm and pointed. Towards the *Neversink*? Towards the wide sea? Or to a place somewhere in the world which no one knew? None of them dared to ask.

Next morning the *Neversink* set sail, while everyone in the Citadel waved goodbye. The whistle blew, Podgy Plum stoked the furnace, Marinka put butter in the frying pan, Timid Thomas dipped his swabs in the clean water and the Little Captain stood behind the wheel, legs astride, his eyes on the horizon.

They sailed without stopping, by the light of the red sun-balloon by day, and by the blue, yellow and green flames of the northern lights at night.

They put in when they reached the Old Watchman in the lighthouse, to return their North Polar clothes, and after that it was straight ahead for home. Home for Marinka, Podgy Plum and Timid Thomas. But for the Little Captain?

'You can come and live with us,' said Marinka.

'With us too!' cried Podgy Plum.

'And I-I will ask my mother,' stammered Timid Thomas.

But the Little Captain shook his head.

Once again a party was held in the little village among the dunes, because the children had returned safely in the *Neversink*.

'Well, Little Captain, here you are again!' said Salty. 'I'll drink a beer to that. Your health! Will you come and live with me?'

But the Little Captain shook his head. Then he made a speech.

'Marinka,' he said, 'you were the bravest, because you sailed into the harbour of the Misty East in the good-luck chest.

'Podgy Plum,' he said, 'you were the strongest, because you kept the *Neversink* going by always stoking up the fire.

'Timid Thomas,' he said, 'you were the best.'

Thomas blinked.

'You are timid, Thomas,' said the Little Captain, 'but thanks to your *helphelphelp* tracks in the sand we found the sons in the south. And thanks to your choosing the wrong signal light, Scurvyboots landed in the good-luck chest.'

Timid Thomas quivered, but not with fear.

'That's how the world goes,' said the Little Captain, 'but reason has nothing to do with it,' and he went outside, into the bright, starry night.

Next morning the *Neversink* had sailed away. The Little Captain had left without a blast from the whistle and with the engine running softly, to sail the wide blue sea. Had he gone to seek the place he came from, or was the *Neversink* his only home?

If that is true, you may see him sailing past one day, when you are standing on the beach. The *Neversink* is a small boat and the Little Captain is always at the helm, steady and sure, his eyes fixed on the horizon.

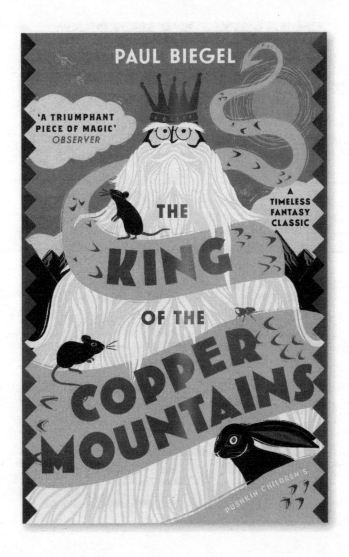

PAUL BIEGEL

'A TRIUMPHANT
PIECE OF MAGIC'
OBSERVER

A
TIMELESS
FANTASY
CLASSIC

THE

KING

OF THE

COPPER
MOUNTAINS

PUSHKIN CHILDREN'S

PAUL BIEGEL
AUTHOR OF THE KING OF THE COPPER MOUNTAINS
AN ENCHANTING FANTASY CLASSIC
THE GARDENS OF DORR
PUSHKIN CHILDREN'S